Caught ON CAMERA

Review

5 stars, Crowned Heart! - InD'tale Magazine

Rachel has dreamed of attending film school for a very long time, and has until the end of the summer to raise the $35,000 tuition to the Toronto Film School. When she lands a job at a resort catering to Hollywood stars, she has hit the jackpot. She can take candid shots of the stars while she is working and sell them to earn her tuition! When a mega-movie star is without a bridesmaid, and Rachel just happens to be the one who can fit the dress without showing up the bride, it is the opportunity of a lifetime. Mickey McNichol, talent agent and best friend of the groom, falls for the beautiful and trustworthy "cousin" of the bride. Will she betray the trust that has been given to her?

Caught on Camera is a super fun read! Full of funny drama and lighthearted banter, it lifts the spirits. Rachel is comical but shy and does not believe she has anything to offer these movie stars or their friends. When she sees they are real people and is accepted by them, her desire to go to film school battles with her integrity. Mickey is a down-to-earth, "tell it like it is" type and takes no prisoners when he wants something, and Rachel is what he wants. A witty, passionate romance, *Caught on Camera* is a great break from reality.

Caught
ON CAMERA

Madelle Morgan

McBride Publishing Group, Canada

Caught on Camera, Hollywood in Muskoka series, Book 1

Published by McBride Publishing Group, 2016

Cover design by Kimberly Killion.
Interior book design and formatting by Tamara Cribley.

Library and Archives Canada
ISBN 978-0-9939881-6-5 (Kindle edition)
ISBN 978-0-9939881-7-2 (epub edition)
ISBN 978-0-9939881-5-8 (Apple Books edition)
ISBN 978-0-9939881-8-9 (paperback)
ISBN 978-1-988917-14-6 (audiobook)

Published in Canada.

This book is dedicated to the hardworking staff of Muskoka resorts, including the now-closed Delawana Inn in Honey Harbour, Ontario, Canada, where I was briefly employed as a chambermaid—my first summer job.

Acknowledgments

Authors blogging at Romancingthegenres.blogspot.ca named two characters. B. A. Binns chose "Juanita Ramirez" for the Reception desk agent, and Sarah Raplee selected "Derek" for Rachel's server friend.

Story editor Lillian Chow asked important questions that precipitated a big rewrite, ultimately making this a much better story. My copy editor, Stacey D. Atkinson, mirrorimagepublishing.ca, took it from there to polish the book.

Kim Killion, thekilliongroupinc.com, not only designed a cover that captures the tone of *Caught on Camera*'s story, she created the brand for the *Hollywood in Muskoka* series.

Inside the cover, formatter Tamara Cribley of deliberatepage.com designed and formatted the content.

Contents

Caught on Camera Review i
Acknowledgments vii
Cast xi
Playlist xii

Chapter 1: Maid in Muskoka 1

Chapter 2: The Princess Bride 9

Chapter 3: Working Guy 15

Chapter 4: The Spa Who Loved Me 22

Chapter 5: Pretty Women 34

Chapter 6: Must Love Police Dogs 45

Chapter 7: Hooked 53

Chapter 8: Splash 68

Chapter 9: What Happens in Muskoka Stays in Muskoka 78

Chapter 10: You've Got Email 84

Chapter 11: There's Something About Rachel 94

Chapter 12: Can Buy Her Love 105

Chapter 13: His Best Friend's Wedding 114

Chapter 14: Gone with the Dog 123

Chapter 15: The Bouquet Hunter 138

Chapter 16: Only You 149

Chapter 17: Sleepless in Muskoka 163

Chapter 18: As Bad as It Gets 174

Chapter 19: How to Lose a Guy in Two Days 179

Chapter 20: 9 ½ Weeks Later. 184

Chapter 21: She's All That 195

Chapter 22: Happy Together .207

Seduced by the Screenwriter Excerpt 216

Books by Madelle Morgan 226
About the Author. 227
Follow Madelle. 228

Cast

(in order of appearance)

Rachel Lehmann: Chambermaid, age 22

Damien "Mickey" McNichol: Groomsman, Hollywood agent, 31

Catherine "Candy" Kane: Bride, 33

Wendy (Wanda) Davila: Candy's personal assistant (PA), 23

Mopette: Candy's Maltese dog, 2

Juanita Ramirez: Reception agent, 21

Angeline Cousineau: Hotel head housekeeper, 48

Marie-Eve Tremblay: Hair stylist and makeup artist, 21

Halden Armstrong: Groom, A-list actor, 32

Tiffany York: Bridesmaid, starlet, 25

Garth Armstrong: Best man & groom's brother, 30

Asta Armstrong: Bridesmaid & groom's sister, 26

Wade Edgeworth: Groomsman, film lawyer, 32

Raynald Donner: Fashion photographer, 35

Derek Witte: Hotel server, 22

Catrina Turner: Security guard, 33

Titan: Retired police service dog, 9

Arjun Chauhan: Hotel general manager (GM), 36

Playlist

Caught on Camera has a soundtrack! When you see this symbol in the chapter [♫], listen to the song that accompanies the story. You'll need to listen on your smartphone, laptop, or another device.

Several songs feature these popular artists born in Canada: Carly Rae Jepsen, Eva Avila, Avril Lavigne, and Michael Bublé.

Listening to songs while reading the story is optional, but if you'd like to try it, here's how:

Option 1: Create a playlist before starting to read the novel
If you subscribe to a music streaming service, create a *Caught on Camera* playlist using the titles of the songs below. Then when you see [♫] together with the title of a song in the text, listen to that song on your device.

Option 2: Madelle Morgan's YouTube playlist
Open YouTube.com in your browser and search for "Madelle Morgan *Caught on Camera*." Click on the playlist entitled "*Caught on Camera*." As you read the novel, when you see [♫] together with the name of a song, listen to it on Madelle's YouTube playlist.

If you can't find the YouTube playlist, go to MadelleMorgan.com/cocplaylist and follow the instructions.

Note: certain songs may not be available in your country on YouTube.com, in the iTunes Store, or from Spotify, Apple Music and other music streaming services.

★★★★★

"Train on a Track," performed by Kelly Rowland, from the film *Maid in Manhattan.*

"The Work Song," from the Disney film *Cinderella.*

"Pretty Girls," performed by Britney Spears and Iggy Azalea.

"I Really Like You," performed by Carly Rae Jepsen, from the album *Emotion.*

"Love Came for Me," performed by Rita Coolidge, from the film *Splash.*

"Damned," performed by Eva Avila, from the album *Give Me the Music.*

"I Wanna Be Loved By You," performed by Marilyn Monroe, from the film *Some Like It Hot.*

"Can't Buy Me Love," performed by Michael Bublé, written by Paul McCartney, from the Bublé album *It's Time.*

"Bridal Chorus (Here Comes the Bride)," processional, composed by Richard Wagner.

"Wedding Day," performed by Seal (duet with Heidi Klum), from the album *System.*

"Wedding March," recessional, composed by Felix Mendelssohn.

"I Wanna Be Loved By You," reprise, performed by Marilyn Monroe, from the film *Some Like It Hot*.

"Once in a Lifetime," performed by Michael Bolton, from the film Only You.

"All of Me," cowritten and performed by John Legend, from the album *Love in the Future*.

"Single Ladies (Put a Ring on It)," cowritten and performed by Beyoncé, from the album *I Am…Sasha Fierce*.

"Nobody Does It Better," performed by Carly Simon, theme from the Bond film *The Spy Who Loved Me*.

"We're in the Money," performed by Ginger Rogers, from the film *Gold Diggers of 1933*.

"Wish You Were Here," performed by Avril Lavigne, from the album *Goodbye Lullaby* (Deluxe Edition).

"Hollywood," cowritten and performed by Michael Bublé, from the album, *Crazy Love*, Hollywood Edition.

Chapter 1

Maid in Muskoka

Rachel rolled the housekeeping cart over the Sterling Inn Muskoka's thick wool hall carpet. Glasses still warm from the dishwasher clinked softly on the lower shelf. Taking a deep breath, she knocked on the door of the first room on her list. She never knew what to expect when she entered a guest room. A couple so engrossed in lovemaking that they didn't hear her knock? A lecherous man who assumed his wealth gave him the right to make a pass at the maid? Or a celebrity who'd be the perfect subject for a candid photo? She guiltily fingered the miniature camera disguised as a chunky pendant on the chain around her neck.

The muffled order, "Come in!" gave her permission to swipe the master key card dangling from the coiled bracelet around her left wrist and enter the $600 a night ground-floor room. Only one side of the king-sized bed had been slept in. On the spacious private terrace overlooking Lake Muskoka, a muscular male figure clad only in tight shorts and running shoes stood outlined against the blazing sun, smartphone to his ear.

He glanced at her. "Would you mind applying sun-screen to my back? The sun is fierce this morning." His casual tone harbored no hint of seduction.

Unfazed, Rachel pushed at the glasses slipping off her nose and stepped through the sliding glass doors to the flagstone terrace. The resort's wealthy, pampered guests expected staff to fulfill every request. This man noticed her shapeless silvery-gray uniform, not her. He merely wanted a favor.

Rarely did she have the opportunity to get this close to a hunky male guest, especially a celebrity. Snagging the bottle of sunscreen on the patio table, she scrutinized his even-featured, smooth-shaven face with its Keanu Reeves-like dark, lean intensity. There was no ring on his left hand holding the smartphone.

Rachel soaked up North American entertainment trivia like the Sahara Desert absorbed water. She recognized most film and television stars. Unfortunately this handsome dude wasn't one of them.

Elsewhere in the luxury inn that morning, staff scurried to prepare for a celebrity wedding. The groom, a Hollywood A-list actor, had booked the Sterling Inn's fifty rooms because paparazzi seldom followed celebrities across the border to Canada's version of the Hamptons. Even so, the groom had hired security guards to patrol the perimeter of the ten acre lakeshore property and adjacent golf course. A speedboat cruised back and forth across the bay, keeping boats with no business at the inn out of telephoto lens range.

Members of the wedding party and guests had begun to arrive the previous day, a Thursday. Juanita Ramirez, the senior front desk agent, or, as the male staff nicknamed the busty beauty, the "hostess with the mostest," spread the word that Ryan Gosling had checked in. Rachel shivered with delight, thrilled she'd scored a summer job as a chambermaid at the celebrity-favored resort.

Cleaning rooms occupied by the rich and famous was her ticket to fulfilling her dream to make movies in Hollywood. She needed $35,000 by September for Toronto Film School tuition. Unfortunately a minimum wage salary for grueling days of manual labor and generous tips from wealthy guests wouldn't cut it. She'd made a plan: secretly snap and sell candid photos of famous guests to the tabloids and entertainment shows. Problem solved.

How lucky am I that the inn will be packed with Hollywood stars this weekend?

And here in front of her was her first chance to score a salable photo. Although she didn't recognize him, the fact that he'd been invited to the wedding implied he was a "somebody." Rachel squirted SPF 30 lotion onto her palms.

The man presented his tanned back to her and continued his call. His dark hair was threaded with premature silver. Her fingers trembled as they neared his body. She spread the lotion on golden, smooth skin. Her senses flooded with awareness of his intense masculinity. Her slick fingertips itched to sink a little deeper into the rippled muscles across the upper back that tapered to a slim waist—no love handles marred this thirtyish hunk. And what a tight butt!

The guest continued to speak into his phone, oblivious of her *very* slow sweeps across his shoulders. "I'll have the contract signed before I leave." He listened for a moment. "Delonda, don't worry. Stall the property manager until Monday. McNichol and Associates is absolutely going to lease that suite." Tension in muscles under her fingers belied the bravado in his voice.

An agitated buzzing emanated from the phone. He chuckled, outwardly unperturbed. "I've got this. You know me, how I operate. She'll be putty in my hands."

Ohhh, she had a thing for strong, confident men. *She* wanted to be putty in his hands. Preferably naked putty.

[♬ "Train on a Track"]

However, the general manager (GM) repeatedly drilled into all employees that fraternizing with the guests was *not* part of the service. To reduce temptation on both sides of guest room doors for hook-ups, the GM made it his unofficial practice to hire plain women as room attendants.

Rachel hadn't stressed about passing *that* test in the job interview. Teased in high school, tall, skinny Rachel Lehmann had no illusions about her appearance. Big dark-rimmed glasses dominated an ordinary oval face framed by long mouse-brown hair. Out of uniform Rachel habitually wore baggy T-shirts, hoodies, and yoga pants to conceal gangly limbs and a chest flatter than Lake Muskoka on a calm day.

Exhaling noisily, the mystery guest ended the call and tucked the smartphone into the pocket of his running shorts. With a quick movement, he grabbed his wallet on the patio table and extracted a twenty, which he passed to her with a nod. "Thanks, kid. I'll go for a run and get out of your way."

After he hopped over the low stone wall separating the room's terrace from the lawn, she reentered the room and flung a pillow into a down-filled armchair. *Damn.* The first potential celebrity she'd gotten close enough to photograph, and her overactive hormones kept her hands busy stroking his muscles instead of pressing the tiny digital camera button. As Rachel stripped the bed, she consoled herself with the prospect of two days of photo ops that lay ahead.

Juanita Ramirez at the front desk would supply this guest's name, let her know if he'd be worth pursuing.

For a photo, that is.

★★★★★

In the Bridal Suite two floors above, Catherine "Candy" Kane, CEO of Candy Kane Cosmetics, squeezed back frustrated tears. Her makeup had taken an hour to apply—she didn't want to ruin it. Instead, she pinched her nose between a freshly manicured forefinger and thumb and counted to ten on a deep exhalation through her mouth.

Wendy, her wide-eyed personal assistant (PA), carried Candy's white Maltese in her arms. "I'll take Mopette for a walk."

"Don't you dare leave me in this crisis," Candy hissed nasally from her perch on a cushioned stool at the mirrored makeup vanity.

"I'll locate the wedding planner." The PA edged toward the door.

"What is she, Wonder Woman? Can she spring my maid of honor from border security at the Toronto airport?" Candy's voice rose. "Well, can she?"

"Your maid of honor never told us about her conviction for driving under the influence. She's not allowed into Canada. Your lawyer and the wedding planner can't do anything," her PA replied reasonably. "Your travel agent booked a flight back to LA. She'll be fine."

"But *I'm* not fine." Candy glared at her. "The wedding photos won't be symmetrical," she snapped. "They'll be ruined." She pinched closed her left nostril, inhaled through the right, then switched to exhale slowly from the left nostril. She'd kill right now for a martini rather than yoga breaths to calm her nerves, but she'd quit drinking alcohol soon after she turned thirty at the first horrifying tinge of rosacea on her cheeks.

The PA clutched Mopette to her breasts like a furry shield, slid one step closer to the double doors, and cautiously ventured a suggestion. "You could ask one of the groomsmen to step aside to even up the numbers."

Candy released her nose to think about it, then shook her head. "Halden's brother is his best man, and the other two men are his *friends*," she emphasized. Her shoulders sagged. "He'd never go for it. Besides, I don't want to upset him, not when—"

"When what?"

"Nothing." Candy took another breath. "Think, dammit. That's what I pay you for!"

The young woman paled and squeezed Mopette so tightly she yipped a protest. "Maybe—maybe *I* could try on the dress?" she ventured.

Candy cast her a withering look. "That's not funny, Wanda."

"Ummm, my name's Wendy." She stuck her chin out bravely.

"I prefer Wanda, as I explained when I hired you last month," Candy snapped. "Get used to it." After another yoga breath, she refocused on the crisis at hand. "You're a *size twelve*, and, what, five foot nothing."

"I'm five three," the PA asserted, flushing a humiliated shade of red.

Candy ignored her. "The wedding is *tomorrow*. Where am I going to find an attractive bridesmaid who'll fit the size four dress up here in the godforsaken Great White North?"

A soft knock saved the PA from replying. As she opened the door, Mopette twisted free and dropped to the carpet. Four stubby legs flashed in a blur as she zipped across the room to hide under Candy's stool.

A chambermaid clad in a platinum uniform with a crisp white collar stepped into the room, arms loaded with a stack of fluffy white towels. "You asked for fresh towels, ma'am?"

Candy waved her free hand toward the bathroom. "Remove the wet towels."

"Certainly."

When the chambermaid returned to the sitting area, Candy noticed her figure and height. She beckoned her over. "Don't leave yet." She peered up at the maid's engraved name tag. "Rachel, how tall are you?"

"Ma'am?"

"Just answer the question."

"Five feet eight inches," came the perplexed response.

Candy rose to nip in excess uniform fabric at the maid's waist and hips. "A perfect size four," Candy mused to no one in particular. She stepped back to assess the girl's features. "Remove those gawd-awful glasses and undo your ponytail."

After Rachel obliged, she was ordered to rotate in place.

"Mind if I inspect your skin?" Without waiting for permission, Candy pulled Rachel over to the window and peered intently at her face. "What are you, twenty?"

"Twenty-two, ma'am," said the mystified Rachel.

Candy's lips twitched into a self-congratulatory smile. The solution to her dilemma had miraculously just walked through the door. "Rachel, I need a bridesmaid, and you'll do."

"Excuse me?" Rachel waggled her head like Mopette did after her bath.

Candy snatched the pile of damp towels out of Rachel's arms and tossed them aside. "If the dress fits, you'll have the honor of being a bridesmaid in my wedding tomorrow. What do you say?"

Stunned beyond speech, Rachel's knees buckled and she sank to the floor.

Chapter 2

The Princess Bride

Ten minutes later, Rachel bit her bottom lip as she regarded her reflection in the Bridal Suite's floor-length mirror. An awed part of her brain struggled to accept the extraordinary image of herself barefoot and clad in an exquisite pale-lilac strapless, tea-length chiffon dress with fitted bodice. The practical part fretted about falling behind schedule. She kept one eye on the digital bedside clock and the other on the ball of white fur rolling over her chambermaid uniform on the unmade bed.

[♬ "The Work Song"]

"I need to call the housekeeper, Ms. Kane. I have rooms to clean."

"Wanda will take care of that," the bride-to-be said airily. She turned to her personal assistant. "Inform the hotel manager that I need Rachel until Sunday."

"Right away." The PA bolted for the exit.

"We booked the entire hotel for the wedding," assured the tall, slender woman with a medley of blond highlights in waist-length hair. "What the bride wants, the bride gets.

Relax and show me a few smiles. Mouth open. Mouth closed. You know the drill."

"Drill?"

"Your smile for the wedding photos. I need to approve it." She grabbed Rachel's bare shoulders and twisted her around for a close-up.

"Photos?" Rachel squeaked. Her heart leaped to her throat. With her beyond-ordinary face and small boobs, she'd stand out among all the beautiful people and not in a good way. "You don't want *me* in your wedding photos, surely?"

Ignoring her protest, Ms. Kane tapped a scarlet, French-tipped nail against her perfect chin. "Mouth closed, I think. Yes, a sweet but sexy smile puts the focus on your big brown eyes."

"Ms. Kane?" Rachel burbled, an embarrassed flush warming her cheeks. "I'm not pretty enough for celebrity photos. I belong *behind* the camera, not in front of it. You need to find someone else—"

As Rachel gestured at the mirror, she caught sight of the tiny white dog on the bed behind them. Its devilish black eyes stared straight at Rachel's backside. To her horror, she noticed a dark stain spreading out from under its butt and over her uniform. "Oh my gods. Your dog just urinated on the bed!"

"Did she?" With Ms. Kane's good humor restored, she merely glanced at her pet sitting innocently beside a puddle rapidly disappearing through Rachel's uniform into the eight-hundred-thread-count Egyptian-cotton duvet cover. "Naughty Mopette," she cooed. "It's Wanda's fault. She's supposed to walk you every four hours. The maid will clean it up."

"*I'm* the maid!"

"Not anymore you're not. This weekend you're my bridesmaid. A distant cousin on my mother's side from…from…"

"Toronto," Rachel supplied.

"Right, Toronto, Canada. Where they have that international film festival."

"And the largest city in Canada," Rachel added dryly.

"So it's settled."

"But"—Rachel flung an arm toward the mirror—"look at us," she wailed. "Standing beside you I'm…I'm the beautiful princess's ugly stepsister."

"Not stepsister," Ms. Kane scolded, wagging a slender, elegant forefinger. "Cousin, remember? And give me some credit for the ability to make you presentable. You must know that I was a model before I launched Candy Kane Cosmetics? It's my business to transform women's faces into the best they can be. A skillful application of makeup, and you won't recognize yourself."

Rachel heaved a tremulous breath, then another. She'd viewed hundreds if not thousands of films, so she knew all about the magical transformation that actors underwent in a makeup artist's chair. All eyes would be on the bride anyway, right?

I'll merely be a secondary character. Not even that—an extra. No one pays attention to walk-ons. I'll be practically invisible. Her galloping pulse slowed.

Taking Rachel's acceptance for granted, Candy Kane's mind was already on a different track. "Don't you *dare* tell any of the guests you work here." Candy swiped fingers across her mouth in a zipping motion. "There's a big tip in it if you keep the secret and pull this off."

How big? Rachel wanted to ask, but kept her "sweet but sexy" lips clamped shut. Truthfully, a generous tip wasn't the reason a shiver of excitement rippled across her exposed skin. Panic receding, she'd belatedly begun to appreciate the photo-taking opportunities associated with being on the set in a supporting role, so to speak, instead of as a hotel employee with no legitimate excuse to approach a celebrity wedding guest.

"I have an idea!" Candy carefully unzipped the bridesmaid's dress. "*You* can walk Mopette this weekend. Wanda is *extremely* busy taking care of a thousand details for me. You already have a key card to the suite, and you won't have anything else to do now that you're working for me." When she noticed Rachel's eyes widen, she amended, "I mean, now that you're doing me this huge favor."

Rachel sighed, resigned. "I suppose if I *don't* walk your little dog she'll do her toilette all over the suite, and guess who will have to clean it up when you check out?"

"Now you're thinking. Step out of the dress."

After Rachel obliged, Candy gathered it up and hung it on its hanger. "Wanda will book you in for hair and makeup in the spa salon early this afternoon and tomorrow before the wedding."

She swept a critical glance over Rachel from head to unpolished toes. "Plan to spend the entire afternoon there today. I want your hair colored a shade that complements mine but doesn't compete with it. I *must* approve the shade first, understand? Let them know you need your brows plucked, lash extensions, mani-pedi, waxing…"

She lifted Rachel's bare left arm to look at the armpit and shook her head in disgust. "Stubble. You actually use a razor? Tell them to wax *everything*."

She ran an exploratory forefinger down Rachel's cheek and then rubbed the skin on the back of her work-roughed hand. "You use *soap*." She tutt-tutted. "At least your dry skin won't be evident in touched-up photos. If there's time, ask for a moisturizing facial. And lose the glasses."

Rachel's insecurity reasserted itself at this brutal description of the amount of work required to make her presentable enough to fit in. "Ms. Kane, are you positive you want *me* in your wedding party?"

"You fit the dress. Besides, a beautiful bridesmaid might steal the spotlight."

Candy's brittle laugh didn't fool Rachel, who held no illusions about her personal appearance and therefore accepted Candy's preference for a plain bridesmaid. "There's no risk of that," Rachel responded grimly.

No doubt it would be a surprise to the arrogant Ms. Kane, but Rachel had never heard of the woman until the announcement of Candy's engagement three months ago to blond heartthrob Halden Armstrong, star of the 3-D epic blockbuster *Apollo: The Battle for Troy* and its sequel *Apollo's Vengeance*.

According to the entertainment news, the third movie in the franchise was scheduled to start shooting in November. But because Candy Kane wasn't in the entertainment business, *People* and the other celebrity news magazines had ignored her until the engagement. When she had a moment, Rachel intended to research every scrap of gossip Google offered up about her "cousin."

"We're done here," Candy said over her shoulder as she carried the dress to the walk-in closet. "You may leave."

Rachel ruefully contemplated her ruined uniform on the soaked bed. "I have nothing to wear."

"We're roughly the same size. Wanda will select one of my outfits for you to wear for the rehearsal at four o'clock, followed by a cocktail hour and dinner tonight."

Then Candy clued in to Rachel's state of *déshabillé*. "Oh, you mean *now*. I suppose you can't run through the hall in your granny panties. Take one of our robes," she invited generously, "but replace it ASAP."

Rachel dashed to the bathroom to retrieve a hotel robe. On her return, she bent to collect the discarded towels on the salon carpet.

Ms. Kane emerged from the closet dangling a pair of lavender pumps from two forefingers. "I almost forgot. Try these on."

Obediently Rachel slipped her feet into the shoes dyed to match the bridesmaid's dress. The three inch heels sank into the thick carpet, and she wobbled to maintain her balance. The pumps squeezed her toes dreadfully, yet were loose at the heels.

"My former maid of honor's shoes fit you," Candy crowed. "The wedding photos will be perfect after all."

Rachel's good fortune to be conscripted into the Kane-Armstrong wedding party and have secret photo-op access to their guests felt like a dream. She pinched herself.

As she gathered up her soiled uniform from the bed, the awful truth hit her. She'd tucked the hidden-camera pendant into the pocket of her pee-drenched uniform.

Chapter 3

Working Guy

Ignoring his bare-chested, sweaty appearance after his morning run, Damien McNichol—Mickey to his friends—strode across the Sterling Inn lobby to Reception. A beautiful dark-haired woman with luminous cognac skin straightened and subtly thrust D-cup breasts toward him. An engraved brushed-nickel tag on the tightly fitted pale-gray jacket with silver buttons supplied her name.

He braced his arms on the marble counter and flashed his best conspiratorial smile. "Good morning, Juanita. Has Tiffany York checked in?"

"Not yet, sir. Shall I have a bellhop locate you when Ms. York arrives? Or if you prefer, I'll take care of it myself." The woman's hooded gaze roamed over his torso, making no secret of her interest in another type of personal service.

Mickey possessed no inclination for casual afternoon delight on this brief trip to Canada to attend an old friend's wedding. Not when Tiffany York held his future in her soft little hands. He withdrew his arms and backed off the counter. To soften the unspoken rejection, he assumed the charming grin he'd perfected in front of a mirror. "If you'd leave a message on my room phone when she arrives, that'll be fine. It's McNichol in room twelve."

The front desk agent masked her disappointment with a sunny smile. "I know who you are, Mr. McNichol." Reverence honeyed her words. "You're a Hollywood agent."

Holy Barracuda. Was there no place in the world a man might escape women who pursued him for ulterior motives? In Juanita, he recognized the too familiar gambit to acquire an "I slept with a Hollywood talent agent" notch on her belt. Or worse, to use him for access to a casting director. Or to shop a screenplay she happened to carry in her handbag. He'd seen it all during ten years in the business of representing minor actors, screenwriters, and members of film crews.

Then his opportunistic brain clicked into gear. This wedding weekend, he was merely one of many men of interest to this buxom beauty at the front desk. With his career on the cusp of jumping to the next level, he needed a clear field to impress Tiffany. Why not deflect the female staff's advances to a more promising candidate, namely his rival for Tiffany's attention?

"Do you know Garth Armstrong?"

"Mr. Garth Armstrong checked in last night, sir. About six foot three, dark blond hair, muscular build?"

"That's him." Mickey leaned in and confided in a low voice, "Garth is the millionaire brother of the groom and runs his film production company." He added with a suggestive wink, "Garth is Hollywood's most eligible bachelor and single at the moment."

Juanita's lush lips puckered into a barely audible "ooooh," and her smoky amber eyes widened. "Thank you, sir."

Mickey slapped a hand on the marble. "You'll inform me the minute Ms. York steps on the property?"

"Certainly, sir. Is there anything else I can do for you?"

"Please have a dozen pink roses sent to Ms. York's room, and charge it to my credit card."

The agent tapped the request into the computer. "The message on the card, sir?"

He pondered a moment, then grinned. "From the man who will make your dreams come true. Mickey."

★★★★★

Clad only in a guest bathrobe over embarrassingly ratty underwear and wearing scuffed rubber-soled tennis shoes, Rachel pushed the housekeeping cart briskly down the corridor past the assigned rooms on her list. She needed to find the head housekeeper fast.

After stowing the cart out of sight in the third floor linen room, she gingerly extracted the camera pendant from her robe pocket, sprayed a cloth with disinfectant, and wiped down the pendant and cord. Although panicked about whether it still worked, she decided that testing must wait until later.

Rachel bolted down the service stairway to the ground floor and along the corridor, zipping past a couple of housekeeping carts parked outside rooms with doors open, coworkers inside stripping beds and vacuuming. This was not the time to answer questions. Finally she reached the housekeeping supply room.

"Angeline! Thank the hospitality gods." Rachel slipped in and shut the door.

Angeline Cousineau, head of housekeeping, scowled and waved her inventory clipboard. "You're supposed to be on third. And what are you doing dressed like that?"

"The GM hasn't told you?" Rachel double-knotted the robe belt that had loosened on her mad dash to the supply room.

Guest complaints to the GM were Angeline's biggest fear. With four young mouths to feed at home, the squat local woman of Native American heritage needed the job. Alarm chased impatience across her face. "What's wrong?"

"The bride, Catherine Kane, insists that I be in her wedding." Details of the situation tumbled out.

Angeline's expression seesawed between disbelief and shock, settling on doubt. "No one told me anything. I'll check with the GM, but meanwhile you"—she waved the clipboard in a scooting motion—"get back to work. I assigned you five turnovers for check-ins, plus four occupied rooms. Did you finish the Bridal Suite?"

Rachel wrung her hands. "That's what I've been trying to tell you. Ms. Kane insisted I try on the bridesmaid's dress. She's still in the suite with her dog. She peed on the bed."

"Ms. Kane?" Angeline registered no surprise. Thirty years in the hotel business, she'd seen the gamut of guest behavior.

"No, her incontinent dog. She ordered me to walk the animal every four hours all weekend."

Angeline's dusky cheeks paled, and not because she cared one bit about the dog. "You haven't cleaned the Bridal Suite? It's almost noon! Which rooms are done?"

Rachel, well aware she'd dropped a bomb into Angeline's orderly world, babbled, "I've only had time to clean twelve and sixteen. Some guests slept in, probably jet-lagged with the three-hour time change between here and California. The Bridal Suite king has to be stripped down to the mattress and a fresh down duvet found for it." Rachel buried her face in her hands. "I'm so sorry."

"Un-be-lievable." Angeline simply stared at her, trying to wrap her mind around the enormity of this disaster. Then her gaze sharpened. "Hey! The robe you're wearing—where's your uniform? If you hooked up with a guest…well, that's a firing offense, and you know it."

"Oh my gods, no! I have *not* been messing around. While I was trying on the bridesmaid's dress to see if it fit, the dog peed on my uniform." She tugged the collar of the cotton robe. "I had to borrow this or run here half-naked."

"You maids are darn lucky there aren't any security cameras in the hotel corridors, or none of you'd last a month," Angeline snapped.

The GM was obsessive about protecting the privacy of his guests and had refused to install digital security cameras inside the hotel. The hotel thus reassured guests that there'd be no record of extramarital dalliances or nocturnal visits to rooms other than their own.

"Misbehaving summer staff are gonna give me a heart attack." Angeline picked up the house phone and punched in the GM's cell number with one stubby forefinger.

He answered immediately. The GM was very efficient. Some less charitable employees called him a micromanager. Still, if anyone knew what was happening in the hotel, he did.

"Mr. Chauhan, one of my room attendants tells me she's been asked to be a bridesmaid in the Kane-Armstrong wedding."

For several moments Angeline listened with dark eyes round, her jaw hanging. "I never heard of such a thing," she finally injected. She rolled her eyes at the ensuing stream of dialogue, and Rachel intuited that Angeline was on the receiving end of one of the GM's infamous lectures on the importance of superb service.

Angeline hung up the receiver. "Mr. Chauhan says the California couple is dropping more than three hundred thousand bucks this weekend, and if they want you to be in the wedding party, you're in. He says he's comping the spa services for you, and to get your ass over there."

"He never said that!"

"Well, he used fancier words, but that's the gist." Angeline wiped the flat of her palm down her cheek. "Jeez Louise. I'll have to pick up the Bridal Suite myself and assign the rest of your rooms to the other room attendants."

Rachel balled her fists. "They're going to hate me."

"You got that right!" Angeline began loading fresh linens onto an unassigned cart. "Where in hell's half acre did I put those extra king duvets?" she mumbled.

Rachel bit on a fingernail before catching herself. The manicurist needed at least a sliver beyond the pink nail bed to work with. "You don't hate me, Angeline, do you? I never asked for this."

Angeline winced. "You want my permission to enjoy hanging out with Hollywood stars for a couple of days while the rest of us do your work? Yeah, the female staff will give you some grief, but any one of those girls would trade places with you in a minute. Matter of fact, twenty years younger, so would I."

The complications of Rachel's new role began to surface. "Ms. Kane wants me to keep this charade on the down-low, but I'm sure to be found out. I don't have any decent clothes to wear when pretending to be a guest."

No bridesmaid of Ms. Kane's would be caught dead in Rachel's faded T-shirts and one-piece racer-back swimsuit, nor the casual summer clothes she might borrow from the other staff.

"Check the lost and found." Angeline indicated the large basket on the shelving unit where the room attendants temporarily stored items left behind. "Now to find Claudette and Jessica and assign them your rooms."

She pushed the cart into the hallway, grumbling under her breath.

Rachel lifted the basket off the shelf and dumped the contents on the floor to dig through the collection of abandoned tops, jackets, sandals, tubes of sunscreen, hats, swim goggles, and other paraphernalia. Finally, she sat back on her heels to regard the limited options: a turquoise halter top and white cotton tennis skirt, a gauzy swimsuit cover-up, and a leopard-print thong bikini bottom and matching top with scraps of triangular fabric so minuscule they made her cheeks burn.

Even if I eventually work on a film set with these Hollywood guests, none of them will remember me, she promised herself silently.

You're out of your league, her conscience whispered.

Rachel squared her shoulders. *I'm no actor, but I can fake this bridesmaid gig. What's so difficult about standing around undercover in fabulous clothes and shoes with a sweet but sexy smile plastered on my face?*

Her conscience instilled doubt. *You'll be a fish out of water. A practically naked fish if you dare to wear that bikini. What if the guests discover you're only a maid?*

That's Ms. Kane's problem, Rachel shot back. The rebuttal silenced her conscience. For a millisecond.

Her intrusive conscience countered with the key issue shredding her nerves: *What if the Kane-Armstrongs discover you've sold photos of their wedding? Halden Armstrong is a powerful man. Your name will be mud in Hollywood.*

Rachel compressed her lips. *I'll never* get *to Hollywood if I can't pay for film school.* She fingered the camera pendant in her pocket with one hand, dangled the risqué bikini top from the other. *I have to risk exposure, in both senses. It's my big chance.*

Chapter 4

The Spa Who Loved Me

Rachel reclined in the spa salon chair and squirmed to position her neck comfortably in the sink notch. Marie-Eve Tremblay, petite, ebony hair pulled back into a chignon, and clad in a formfitting platinum tunic that barely covered her rear end, turned on the spray and tested the water temperature.

"You will not know your face when I finish," Marie-Eve promised in her sexy French-Canadian accent. She normally worked as a hair stylist and makeup artist in the high-end spa at the Sterling Inn Montreal, but she had swung a four-month transfer to the Sterling Inn Muskoka property to perfect her English.

Ms. Kane's PA had come and gone, leaving behind instructions for hair color. She'd emailed a two-day schedule to Rachel, complete with designated times to walk the dog.

Marie-Eve rinsed the color solution out of Rachel's hair. "Very beautiful, long blond hair, *ma belle*. When it is dry, you will see. Your skin is too pale, though. No sun."

"I usually work extra shifts on my days off." Blissfully happy, Rachel sniffed the floral scent wafting through the air. She'd scraped by on minimum wage and tips since moving out of her divorced mother's modest apartment at nineteen, worked long hours to pay her way through community college, and never aspired to be pampered with spa services that cost the earth.

Marie-Eve applied conditioner with soothing fingers. "You are saving money for something?"

"I've been accepted at Toronto Film School. It's very expensive."

"Then I don't receive a tip from you today." Marie-Eve laughed. "It's okay. You will remember me when you're famous, and I can do *maquillage* for the cinema stars."

"Speaking of makeup, what's your professional opinion of the Candy Kane line of cosmetics?"

"Naturally the spa ordered a stock for the wedding party and guests." Marie-Eve indicated the red-and-white-striped packaged products on a shelf. "I have tried it before in Montreal. We test all the new products to compare to the Sterling spa line." She shrugged. "It's organic. It's as good as others in that price range. We stay with our spa products."

"I never heard of Candy Kane Cosmetics until this week," Rachel admitted.

Marie-Eve finished rinsing the conditioner from Rachel's long hair, then wrapped a towel embroidered with the hotel logo around her wet head and guided her to a swivel chair in front of a mirror.

"Makeup is very competition."

"Competitive," Rachel automatically corrected.

"*Oui.* Candy Kane advertises on the Shopping Channel. The packaging is for adolescents. New products, they come and go." Marie-Eve wrapped a fresh, dry towel around Rachel's neck, followed by a plastic cape. "Could be a success. Maybe not." She shrugged her shoulders.

"Ms. Kane was a model," Rachel offered.

In the mirror Marie-Eve's reflection tilted her head to inspect Rachel's long hair, comb at the ready. "I am twenty-one, about your age, *n'est-ce pas*? We are too young to see her photos in the magazines *de mode*. At thirty-three she is still very beautiful, but maybe too old to model."

"Fashion magazines," Rachel corrected. She grimaced at her reflection. "Washed up at thirty-three. Yikes. The fashion industry sure is heartless."

She began to comb out Rachel's hair. "Hollywood too. A fan of Goldie Hawn's was here last week. She said Goldie Hawn's character in *The First Wives Club* says: 'There are only three ages for women in Hollywood—Babe, District Attorney, and *Driving Miss Daisy*.'"

Rachel smiled ruefully. "If you replace 'district attorney' with 'business woman,' then Ms. Kane has moved into the next age." She changed the subject. "Can you tell me anything about the other members of the wedding party?"

Marie-Eve efficiently snipped off half an inch of wet hair to even the length. "I know nothing of the men. The personal assistant, Wendy Davila, arranged appointments tomorrow for bridesmaids' hair and makeup. Asta Armstrong is the groom's sister, *je crois*. Tiffany York is another bridesmaid."

Rachel nodded. "Tiffany is a model turned actress. I read on Variety.com that she auditioned to be the next Bond girl. She must be one of Candy's model friends."

Marie-Eve switched on a handheld dryer and began to blow-dry the long strands. "Tiffany is very beautiful, *comme tu dis*, 'a babe.' I watch on *Entertainment Tonight* that she is divorcing the director who put her in his movie, it was two years ago. She does not require that old guy anymore for her career. He is forty years, I think."

"Old," Rachel corrected.

"Yes. Very old."

"Forty years *old.*" Rachel smiled. "Forget it."

Marie-Eve killed the blow-dryer. "*Tiens.* Blond hair accents the sparks of gold in your brown eyes. Ms. Kane has an expert eye."

An unfamiliar blond woman squinted at her from the wall mirror. Rachel fumbled under the cape for the glasses in her robe pocket and put them on. *Whoa. Shapeshifter metamorphosis.* Her own mother would pass her on the street.

Marie-Eve made a moue of distaste. "You must wear those ugly glasses?"

Rachel sighed. "I'm blind as a bat. I need glasses to see farther than ten feet. To save money I never reordered contacts when I ran out."

"This weekend is special. You must put those glasses away," Marie-Eve ordered firmly, removing the plastic cape and shaking it. "Now you will have a light lunch in the atrium with the other spa clients before Claire, the esthetician, shapes your brows, dyes and lengthens your lashes, and waxes your private parts. The fun stuff."

★★★★★

Two hours later Rachel emerged from the lobby elevator wearing the turquoise halter top and white cotton tennis skirt, and feeling as if she'd switched bodies with a glamorous, sexy stranger. Her body burned "down there" where Claire had energetically ripped strip after strip from waxed skin. A Brazilian, she'd called it. Rachel called it torture.

Mopette waggled happily on a leash behind her. They scooted across the polished wood floor to the entrance as fast as her black flip-flops and the white dog's short legs allowed, camera pendant bouncing on her chest and a white plastic poop bag clutched in her hand.

The doorman pulled open the door and tipped his head. "Ma'am."

"Thank you, George."

He did a double take as Rachel scooched past him. She trotted across the parking lot, positioned the leashed dog on the manicured lawn, and waited.

And waited.

"Do your business, you little—" A middle-aged man in a golf shirt approached a Porsche convertible and eyed her appreciatively. "Darling pet," she amended.

Mopette did not squat. Rachel waited some more, shifting her weight impatiently from foot to foot. The car left, and an airport limo pulled up to the entrance. Rachel strained to identify the couple exiting the limo. Mopette strained against the leash in the direction of the lush green open spaces of the hotel's eighteen-hole golf course. At a distance of thirty feet, without her glasses, for all she knew the blurry arrivals were assistants rather than celebrity guests. She aimed the camera pendant in their general direction anyway, snapping pictures until the figures disappeared through the front entrance.

Mopette tugged on the leash, alternately yapping and sniffing fresh, humid air through a twitching black button nose pointed at the golf course. Perhaps finicky, spoiled Mopette required privacy.

Fine. She wrapped the leash around one wrist and let Mopette lead the way slowly up a stone-dust path toward the ninth fairway. The little dog trotted happily, its tiny pink tongue hanging out of the side of its mouth, the red-and-white-candy-striped bow askew behind one ear. Upon reaching the rough at the edge of the rolling vista of groomed grass, Mopette tugged Rachel in the direction of a water hazard.

"Are you thirsty, Mopette?" Rachel hadn't thought to bring water. Wishing for her glasses, she squinted up the green fairway in a vain attempt to check for golfers. Mopette made a beeline to the rushes at the water's edge and yipped, her short tail with its white plume wagging with excitement. A splash alerted Rachel to a big old turtle swimming across the small pond. She laughed. "Maybe I like walking you after all, Mopette." Strolling outdoors on a sunny June afternoon sure beat cleaning toilets.

An electric golf cart carrying two men crunched over the pebbled path adjacent to the fairway and stopped.

"That looks like Candy's dog," the passenger said.

"Mopette," the driver called in a deep voice.

Obediently Mopette lifted short legs from wet muck and yanked Rachel toward the visitors. While Rachel's attention was distracted, Mopette had ventured deeper into the weeds bordering the pond. *Oops.*

She drew close enough to recognize Halden Armstrong at the wheel.

Oh my gods! The A-list star who owned his own film production company appeared more gorgeous in person than in photos in the entertainment blogs she followed. She froze, hitched a breath, and held it. Her first celebrity in the flesh. She'd seen all his movies, of course. He *owned* the screen in every scene.

Halden unfolded long legs and levered his six feet six inches from the cart. The blond Adonis, with piercing blue eyes and muscular build reminiscent of Chris Hemsworth, supplied a blindingly sexy smile that reputedly had caused teenage girls to faint. No doubt he expected her to explain what she was doing with Candy's dog. She scrabbled for appropriate words. He probably had no idea she'd be walking down the aisle ahead of his bride.

"Ms. Kane—" She caught herself. *Cousins use first names.* "Candy asked me to walk the dog."

"Typical," proclaimed Halden's passenger in the golf cart.

Ignoring his golf partner, Halden offered her a hand the size of a dinner plate. "My name's Halden Armstrong. And yours?"

"Rachel Lehmann, sir, I mean, Mr. Armstrong." She switched the leash to her left hand and held out her right. His hand gently enfolded hers like a baseball glove before releasing it. "I may never wash this hand again," she blurted without thinking.

He raised his chiseled chin and laughed, clearly in an excellent mood. "Hey Mick, I have a fan way up here in Canada." To her, he invited, "Call me Halden." He gestured with his thumb over his shoulder at the shadowed figure in the golf cart. "That's Mickey McNichol, the agent who launched my career. He's one of my groomsmen."

The other man climbed out of the golf cart and approached them. *Eeep.* Mickey was the guest she'd slathered with sunscreen that very morning. *Does he recognize me?* Her heart tip-tapped under the skimpy top.

Dwarfed beside the easygoing groom with the superhero body, Mickey appeared shorter than his actual five foot eleven height. His dark gray eyes snapped with controlled irritation at the interruption of their golf game. His lean physique pulsed with contained energy. She felt a pull, and not from the leash. Her hands itched to stroke those taut muscles hidden under his shirt.

Dimly she realized Halden was speaking. "Mick, Candy texted me an hour ago about Rachel, her Canadian cousin who's stepping in to replace the missing bridesmaid."

Mickey's assessing gaze smoothly raked her body from freshly dyed blond hair to passion pink polished toes without any sign of recognition. "Pleasure to meet a cousin of Candy's, Rachel." He took her hand and gave it a hearty shake. "Let's have a drink after the rehearsal. Speaking of which"—he briskly addressed Halden, who rubbed the underside of Mopette's chin with the toe of his golf shoe—"it's three-thirty. We need to shower before the rehearsal starts at four."

"Relax." Halden waved a hand to dismiss the urgency in Mickey's voice. "They can't start without me. Besides, I've got a hundred bucks on the game and I'm winning. Rachel, may we give you a lift to the clubhouse?"

Rachel was about to accept when she spied Mopette's muddy brown stumps. "Oh my gods!" she yelped. "Candy will be furious."

Halden's deep, throaty chuckle echoed across the fairway. "Candy treats that dust mop like a toy instead of a live animal. I'm happy to see it have fun for a change." He aimed a wickedly amused grin at her and winked.

Dazzled, Rachel forgot to breathe. *This*, she told herself, *is star power.*

"Don't worry," Halden continued. "Wendy's a sport. Sneak Mopette into a bathroom, and she'll hose her down." He climbed back into the golf cart. "Catch you later."

Halden was *real*, Rachel decided. A truly nice guy, despite his fame and fabulousness. But it was Mickey who'd made her heart pitter pat. His intense energy tugged her like metal to Magneto of the *X-Men* movies.

The men zoomed off in the electric cart, silhouetted against the dazzling sun in cloudless sky above the tops of spear-like pines lining the fairway.

She had to shower and change in time for the rehearsal too. Rachel looked down at her charge sitting proudly beside a ribbon of poop. "Good dog! Halden likes you, so you must not be such a bad dog after all."

After using the plastic bag to gingerly collect all evidence of Mopette's toilette, she gave the leash a sharp tug. "Let's go." Mopette whined and planted her tush on the grass, apparently tuckered out by her big adventure. "No, I will not pick you up. You need a bath. I can't return a filthy dog to Wendy or Ms. Kane."

★★★★★

Wracked with guilt for tracking dirt onto spotless linoleum floors she had no time to mop, Rachel dragged the protesting muddy dog from the back entrance and along a service corridor to the housekeeping supply room, where she set Mopette down in the deep janitor sink. Behind her the door swung open.

"Excuse me, miss. Guests aren't allowed in here."

Without turning her head, she called out, "It's all right, Angeline. It's just me." Rachel rinsed one filthy paw and then the other under a stream of warm water. Muddy water swirled down the drain. She scrunched her nose at the smell of wet dog. *Ughh.*

"Rachel?" Angeline queried over a cascade of aggrieved barks. "Let me look at you."

Obediently Rachel stepped away from the sink. She twirled around the room, arms outstretched.

"Hoo, boy. You're beaut-ti-ful! Who'd a thought one afternoon in a spa makes such a difference?"

"Thanks a lot!" Rachel smiled to show she wasn't offended. "I'm having so much fun, except for this minute," she admitted, returning to the unhappy dog. Its little nails scritch-scratched on metal as paws slipped and skidded for traction in the deep, wet sink.

Finally she wrapped both hands around its body and held its tummy under the faucet to sluice off dirt stubbornly clinging to the fur. Yipping incessantly, four black paw pads waving frantically in the air, Mopette rebelled at the indignity.

"Calm down, you little fur ball." Rachel swore colorfully. "You've splattered my halter top with dirty water." This miniature dog, not even ten pounds soaking wet, created an outsized amount of trouble.

Angeline hadn't finished. "You're too pretty to work as a room attendant."

Rachel hooted. "You're just being nice. Please hand me a towel?"

Angeline pulled a white bath towel from the stack on a shelf and tossed it to her. "No, seriously. You *are* too pretty to work in the rooms. Remember the GM's policy?"

"Yip, yip, yip!" Mopette barked in agreement, shook her body, and flung droplets of water on the walls, the floor, Rachel—everywhere.

Rachel wrapped her cozily in the thick towel and lifted her out of the sink. She peered at her reflection in Mopette's glassy little black eyes, her heart plummeting to the pit of her stomach. "Too pretty? I've never been too pretty in my life."

"I expect you've never soaked up hundreds of dollars in spa services in one afternoon either."

"You really think my job is on the line? I'll return to being plain old Rachel on Sunday."

"Won't matter," Angeline gloomily predicted. "After the GM gets a look at you, he'll want you far away from the guest rooms—assign you to the laundry, maybe." Angeline's broad face creased in a dark scowl. "If you're lucky."

Yikes. A summer slaving in the stifling hot laundry room with no tips? A fate worse than being fired. Fired or banished to the service wing, either way she'd forfeit future opportunities to take photos of celebrity guests at Sterling Inn that summer. Tears pricked her eyelids. Candid pics from the Kane-Armstrong wedding were her *only* chance for acquiring enough money for tuition. A tear slid through eyelashes stiff with mascara and dripped blackly on Mopette's white fur.

Star struck upon meeting Halden, she'd completely forgotten to take photos of him on the golf course. How stupid. Another sooty tear dotted Mopette's back.

Suck it up, she ordered herself. It wasn't too late to take photos. The evening cocktail event, rehearsal dinner, and wedding day offered wonderful opportunities. Rachel vigorously rubbed dry Mopette's short legs and tummy. The reward outweighed the risk of suffering the wrath of the Kane-Armstrongs, should they eventually discover who sold the photos. Or so she convinced her conscience.

Fierce ambition to work on a Hollywood film set had flared upon her first visit to a movie theater at the age of five. "I'm going to be in the movies," she'd announced to her mother. But in high school, the pretty, popular girls won lead roles in plays, and boys ignored Rachel, reinforcing a belief that her ordinary features, awkward height, mouse-brown hair, and lack of boobs crushed any chance of joining the ranks of beautiful screen starlets.

At sixteen, all hope of filling a bra withered and died. She abandoned the childish dream of becoming an actress. Instead, she researched film crew jobs that provided the opportunity to spend time on set with the actors and filmmakers she idolized. Of the on-set professions tapped to make a film, directors and camera operators enjoyed mandatory front row seats for the entire shoot. Rachel was a practical person who had to support herself. She calculated that the odds of being hired as an entry-level camera assistant were considerably better than those of becoming a director.

After years of zealously watching hundreds of films, *Entertainment Tonight*, *ET Canada*, and televised *Academy Awards* and *Golden Globe Awards*, the desire to become a camera operator, maybe even a cinematographer someday, burned just as brightly. Only eighteen months at film school stood between cleaning up after movie stars and filming them. And the small matter of $35,000, of course.

I'll do whatever is necessary to work in Hollywood. Rachel heaved a fortifying breath, mustered every ounce of courage, and firmly instructed herself to start clicking that hidden-camera button, consequences be damned.

Chapter 5

Pretty Women

Mickey vaulted over the stone terrace wall outside his room and strode across the inn's manicured front lawn to a white gazebo—a ten foot-diameter round wood platform with a cone-shaped roof supported by four columns—framed against a backdrop of blue sky and water. Off to the right, men and women lounged in the late Friday afternoon sun beside an infinity pool that, from his perspective, seemed to disappear into the vast lake beyond.

The wedding party gathered for the rehearsal at the top of wide granite slabs that stepped down to a sandy beach. He scanned the cluster of well-dressed men and women for Tiffany York. No doubt she planned to make an entrance. He knew his starlets. She wasn't an upcoming actor in his stable yet, but he intended to rectify that before Sunday's departure.

Meanwhile he made himself agreeable, first to those he knew—Halden, his parents, sister Asta, and brother Garth from Wisconsin, clustered together in a tight family circle—and then introduced himself to those he had yet to meet. The tall, slender, elegant middle-aged couple expensively attired in black he identified as Candy's parents. Candy and her estranged twin, Gwendolyn, winners of the genetic lottery, grew up in New York City where their father ran a modeling agency. The parents held champagne flutes by the stems and made polite conversation, but their eyes strayed often to the hotel entrance, watching for Candy to emerge.

He excused himself when the Armstrong family pastor approached the bride's parents, and drifted over to shake hands with Wade Edgeworth, Halden's college roommate and other groomsman. Wade was an entertainment attorney hired on a project basis by studio producers and independent filmmakers. Mickey and Wade often teamed with a favorite independent producer to get a movie financed, also known as green-lighted, by a major studio. Mickey packaged the stars and director, Wade negotiated the financing deals, while the producer developed the screenplay and assembled the preproduction, production, and postproduction teams.

Candy's blond cousin, in a short royal blue shift and sky-high heels that showcased exceptional legs, lingered behind the gazebo in an attempt to make herself inconspicuous. A Californian, he was accustomed to beautiful women, but this girl lacked their casual confidence. She gripped the stem of a half-empty champagne glass in one fist, and the other fiddled nervously with a necklace pendant.

To pass the time awaiting Candy and Tiffany's big entrance, he slid up alongside. "Enjoying yourself?"

She stiffened. "Yes, sir."

"Mickey, please."

She smiled. "Mickey."

He froze. When her pink rosebud lips curled up, unusual gold-flecked brown eyes crinkled at the corners—a genuine smile. Not one he often witnessed in his line of business.

"It's a lovely afternoon." She lifted the champagne glass to her cute mouth.

"Yes." *Lovely. Not the right word for Rachel. Intriguing. And those legs!* He was a leg man, had been since his sister Nikki played with a poseable Barbie doll and GI Joe when they were kids. Nikki had a thing for military men in consequence. Imprinting, that's what it was, but who cared?

Mickey forgot about circulating. Rachel was a stranger to most of the guests, so he devoted the next five minutes to naming the persons waiting for the bride.

"Halden often says that fishing the northern lakes with his brother Garth, Wade, and me keeps him sane."

"What does his sister do?"

Mickey caught on that Rachel obviously wasn't interested in fishing, at least not for fish. Fishing for gossip was more her line. "Asta? She's a stunt double. She's fearless. Fast cars, fast boats, you name it, she can drive it. She's one of my clients. I signed her a couple of years ago."

"Signed her to—"

"I'm an agent," he clarified. "I work for Herron Talent Agency." He left unsaid his plan to launch his own firm. One big name client on his roster, and he'd be able to afford to quit his job and sign the lease on a small but ludicrously expensive suite of offices.

Revelation of his profession to women he met in LA usually sparked calculated interest in his connections, not in him. He braced for a request for access to a particular producer, casting agent, or director.

Rachel tipped her head to regard him, her big gold-flecked eyes serious. "How did you become a talent agent?"

"Long story." Her unexpected personal question left him at a loss for words, triggering an unfamiliar sensation in his gut. He warned himself to focus on his pursuit of

Tiffany, not allow himself to be distracted by a shy girl as skittish as a long-legged filly.

Mickey rarely met a woman who wasn't in the entertainment business or aspiring to be in the business. He didn't mind being used. Hell, he often enjoyed the perks. But by his thirties, casual sex had lost its allure. The gorgeous women were only interested in what he could do for their careers, and dumped him once they got it. Other men called him lucky. He called it lonely.

The hotel door opened, cutting off further conversation. Arm in arm, Candy and Tiffany stepped carefully in stiletto heels along the uneven granite flagstone path to the wedding party scattered around the gazebo. Since Candy didn't drink, he figured Tipsy Tiffany was responsible for their swaying gait. Candy's ever-present assistant Wendy and the middle-aged wedding planner trailed in their wake. Availing himself of the chance to take Tiffany off Candy's hands and into his, Mickey excused himself, handed his champagne flute off to a server, and hurried to intercept the women.

Garth Armstrong reached them first, casually elbowing Mickey aside with the unconscious assertiveness of a former college football player for whom finesse was a foreign concept. "Tiffany, allow me to escort you to the gazebo," Garth growled. For a reason inexplicable to Mickey, women found Garth's rumbling baritone seductive.

Smoothly, as if it had been his intention all along, Mickey offered his arm to Candy. Her natural five foot ten height, augmented by five-inch heels, exceeded his own. He scanned her appreciatively. No woman he knew wore couture as well as Candy. A short cream sheath hung from thin straps, clung to small, perfect breasts, and revealed long, lean thighs. Silky blond hair flowed down a bare back to her waist. She wore no jewelry except the rock Halden put on her ring finger three months earlier.

"You're stunning, Candy. Halden's the luckiest guy in the world."

Like all women, Candy enjoyed genuine appreciation. She patted his forearm, though her gaze roamed in search of her fiancé. "Thanks, darling."

"It's your moment."

"Don't let Tiffany spoil it." Crystal hardness glinted in topaz eyes that had graced countless magazine covers in her day. "She helped herself to my minibar behind my back as I dressed. Ask the waiter to substitute sparkling water for champagne when serving her, will you?"

"I'm on it." Any excuse to stick close to Tiffany was fine by him. Although he had competition. Mickey frowned as Garth walked ahead, a meaty arm wrapped possessively around Tiffany's matchstick waist. Mickey's strategic brain flipped through ideas to waylay Tiffany before she began to reciprocate Garth's interest. He steered Candy toward her groom.

Halden enthusiastically clasped his bride's slim fingers and leaned in to kiss her fervently. "You look gorgeous, babe."

"Darling." Candy wrapped her fingers halfway around his bulging biceps and pressed her upper body into his broad chest for the kiss. Happiness enhanced her ethereal beauty. The cynic in Mickey reluctantly stood down. Against all odds, this Hollywood marriage appeared to be based on true love.

The middle-aged wedding planner, slim, cool, and monochrome in a tailored skirt and jacket of a glossy white fabric the color of her shoulder-length hair, stepped in front of the couple. "It's time for the rehearsal, ladies and gentlemen." She shepherded the family and guests to their places.

★★★★★

After the rehearsal, the wedding party drifted across the lawn to the flagstone terrace for the welcome cocktail hour. Within half an hour, close to a hundred immaculately groomed wedding guests clad in summer-weight suits and a rainbow of summer dresses mingled or clustered around the open bar near the French doors. Servers in crisp white shirts and black trousers circulated with silver trays of prosciutto-wrapped scallops, enormous shrimp on skewers, and caviar on wafers.

Mickey recognized most of the guests by sight if not by acquaintance. He mingled, exchanging a few words with each before moving on. The male Wisconsin relatives in dark jackets sweated in the late-afternoon sun and clutched beer bottles, having rejected the bartender's frosted glasses. Their wives and girlfriends giddily eyeballed celebrities they'd only seen on screen. Raynald Donner, Candy's skeletal fashion photographer friend, slithered between the assembled guests wielding a camera. Candy must have asked Raynald to snap photos of the guests. Mickey knew the wedding planner had arranged for a professional photographer to take official wedding photos.

Mickey searched for Tiffany and spied her seated beside Garth at a small marble-topped table overlooking the lake, her delicate hand encased in a possessive paw. He scowled, his brain busy inventing a plausible errand to remove Garth from the field.

[♫ "Pretty Girls"]

Halden strolled over to his side, a bottle of beer in his left hand. "Tiffany's a train wreck," he observed. After tilting the cold one to his mouth and swallowing a long draught, he continued. "I love Candy, but why she surrounds herself with women friends who can't hold their liquor, I do *not* understand."

Mickey shrugged. Privately, he believed Candy had her own reasons for cultivating friendships with the California "in" crowd. No one knew better than Mickey what it took to make it to the top. He respected Candy's drive and clever head for business, but acknowledged to himself that fierce ambition in anyone, male or female, made him wary. He'd seen too many people compromise their morals in order to succeed. Because Candy had cut her teeth in the high-stakes fashion industry, Mickey knew she'd have no trouble surviving or even thriving in the shark-infested Hollywood pool. He crossed his fingers that his buddy Halden wasn't being used to gain admission into that pool.

Aloud, he said to Halden, "It's Hollywood. The young stars can't handle the pressure to be perfect. They turn to alcohol or drugs."

"Asta refuses to hang with Candy's friends, thank the Lord."

Not that Asta has a choice, Mickey reflected to himself. Asta's wholesome features, sturdy fit physique, and stunt-professional job didn't put her in the same league as the whisper-thin knockouts with boob jobs who climbed over each other to be cast in the few roles available, and often burned out quickly in the hot glare of publicity. Mickey said only, "Adrenaline is Asta's drug of choice."

"She's a daredevil, all right. Keeps Mom up at night worrying." Halden took a swig from the brown longneck bottle and shook his head. "Women."

Tiffany's slim hand fluttered to beckon a server. "Seems like Tiff wants a refill. I should get over there."

Halden clapped a free hand on his shoulder. "Relax. I asked Garth to take Tiffany under his wing this weekend to keep her away from the booze at least until after she walks down the aisle ahead of Candy. You're off the hook."

"Wonderful, just wonderful." Mickey absently patted the inside jacket pocket where he'd stashed an agency contract in anticipation of getting Tiffany alone. Halden knew all about his goal to sign Tiffany before Mickey's boss finished negotiating a Herron Talent Agency contract with Tiff's manager. They'd discussed it that afternoon on the golf course.

Noticing Mickey's expression, Halden added, "Hey, buddy, I thought I was doing you a favor. Candy's cousin is hot!" He tagged Rachel with his chin.

The leggy blonde chatted comfortably with Halden's mother while avidly observing the curated assembly of Hollywood actors, directors, producers, and their partners. Halden didn't care about status or fame. He'd insisted on inviting only friends and relatives to share his big day. It just so happened that many of his friends owned Oscars and Golden Globe awards.

Halden continued. "Anyhow, an agency contract signed by someone who's drunk isn't legal, am I right?"

"Even if it were legal, it'd certainly be morally problematic," Mickey admitted, disappointed all the same. "Should Garth succeed in sobering up Tiffany, and without that barracuda of a manager breathing down her neck, I'm counting on convincing Tiff to sign with my new agency."

"If Tiffany's smart she'll be begging *you* rather than the other way round. Everyone in the business knows that it was you, not your smarmy boss, who called in some favors and arranged her audition for the Bond-girl role."

"Ralph Herron is tight with Tiff's manager. That's why they're cutting me out of the 15 percent agency commission."

Halden raised his brows. "Herron and Tiffany's manager are having an affair? Isn't that a conflict of interest?"

Mickey huffed. "The word is Tiffany York doesn't give a damn which ass her manager kisses, as long as Tiff gets primo parts and a fat paycheck."

Halden shook his head sadly. "Hollywood."

"Yeah."

Halden and Mickey tipped back their heads and drank deeply in unison.

★★★★★

Wendy, with the weekend schedule on a tablet apparently superglued to her left hand, approached Rachel. "It's seven-fifteen. You have time to walk Mopette before dinner at eight."

Grateful for the reason to escape, Rachel immediately made her excuses to Mrs. Armstrong and her friendly daughter, Asta. On her way to the hotel entrance, she absently snagged an enormous shrimp on a skewer from a passing server's tray. She'd been too nervous to eat appetizers in front of the guests, and her stomach gurgled loud enough to be heard over the conversational hum.

Derek Witte, a friend she'd made among the summer waitstaff, called after her. "Rachel? What—"

Rachel screeched to a halt, teetering on five-inch designer stilettos. "Shhhhh." She swung her head left and right to gauge whether nearby guests noticed their exchange. With the coast relatively clear, in a low, urgent voice she revealed, "I've been asked to replace a missing bridesmaid. Ms. Kane wants it kept secret."

Derek snorted through his infamously nosey nose. "Yeah, right." He appreciatively surveyed her from dyed hair to black heels with a gleam in his eyes she'd never noticed before. “You sure do clean up well. I can’t believe you had the nerve to crash this party.”

“Please keep your voice down!” she hissed. Her heart thumped so hard the camera pendant bounced on her chest. “I swear it’s the truth. Check with the GM or Angeline, but otherwise keep it to yourself.”

“I will.” Her tall, occasional jogging companion eagerly loped in the direction of the kitchen, his tray half full.

She groaned. Gossip flashed through the hotel faster than lightning thanks to Derek, the most relentless snoop on the premises. He should be studying to be a police detective, not a biochemist.

Then Mickey stepped forward. Sharp, observant Mickey. The very last person she wanted to witness her exchange with the server.

“What did you say to make him step so lively?” Mickey’s gaze followed Derek’s rapidly retreating back.

Dizziness spun her thoughts. Hanging out with the rich and famous under the hot sun on an empty stomach took its toll, but stress ramped up stratospherically in Mickey’s presence. Physical attraction warred with heart-clenching fear that he’d clue in to the camera pendant and catch her sneaking photos, or that he’d recognize her from that morning in his room.

“Rachel, are you all right?” He placed a warm palm on her bare shoulder to steady her.

Her knees weakened at the contact. Mickey-lust swamped her senses. She remembered to breathe and improvised an answer. “We spoke about…about dog food.” Hurriedly she added, “I have to feed and walk Mopette. Excuse me.” She attempted to squeeze between him and Ryan Gosling’s partner, who was stunning in a low-cut red halter dress.

Mickey adroitly moved to block her escape and pointed at the skewer in her hand. "The dog eats shrimp?"

"No. She eats special food. It's in the Bridal Suite," she babbled. Then, to her horror, he offered to accompany her. Rachel gasped. "No! I mean…that's not necessary. Stay and enjoy the event. Please, sir. I mean, Mickey."

An intrigued grin spread across Mickey's face, and raised the hair on her skin. "Oh, I rather think I'd enjoy spending time with you."

Chapter 6

Must Love Police Dogs

Rachel inserted her master key card into the Bridal Suite lock and pushed open the door. Mickey tagged at her stiletto heels. Mopette wriggled off a puffy pink doggy bed and trotted over to greet and sniff them. A fresh red-and-white-striped satin bow perched between alert ears.

Rachel bent to stroke her fluffy fur. "Hello, Mopette. Where's your leash?"

"It's on the bureau," Mickey said. "I'll get it."

Rachel followed a trail of shredded toilet tissue across the carpet to a chewed-up roll on the bathroom floor. "Oh, you bad dog. What a mess." Automatically she dropped to her knees to pick up the debris.

"Let the maid deal with it," Mickey advised.

"I'm the—" She caught herself. "I'll call housekeeping." As she rose to her feet, a spike heel sank into the plush bath mat and threw her off balance.

"Allow me." Mickey grasped her elbow.

She clung to his forearm and he pulled her upright. Musky aftershave scent wafted her way. The gleam in steel-gray eyes proclaimed he enjoyed the contact. Tingling swept from her hand through to her breasts. Thank heavens she'd worn her own practical cotton bra, or erect nipples would surely have tentpoled the borrowed dress's thin silk material. Magnetically handsome, Mickey inspired lustful feelings. *No*, she told herself. *The weekend's complicated enough already.* She firmly shoved Mickey-lust down.

Mickey held on to her arm for an eternity, watching her face as he said, "Tell me why a beautiful woman like you has trouble walking in heels."

"Canadian girls don't wear high heels," she improvised. "We need to be able to run from the wildlife."

"There aren't any wild animals around here."

"Oh, I spied a wolf or two downstairs."

Mickey chuckled and released her arm.

She looked down at Mopette's handiwork in dismay. If Candy returned to a suite in this condition and the GM ever found out, he'd have a fit. Rachel made a quick call to housekeeping, then collected Mopette's thin white leather leash from Mickey and snapped it onto the matching white leather collar sparkling with *faux* diamonds.

Mickey crossed his arms. "Don't people normally feed the dog before walking it?"

"Right." Flustered, Rachel towed the leashed dog to the bar that doubled as a kitchenette, opened the minifridge, and extracted a pink bowl containing a small can with a pop-top lid. She pried it open, dumped the gourmet contents into the bowl, and set it down on the carpet beside a bowl of water. "Ummm, yummy. Eat your din-din, Mopette."

Mopette sat on tiny haunches, her shiny black eyes aimed up at Rachel expectantly.

Rachel shoved a strand of hair behind her ear and grimly contemplated the persnickety beast. "What now, you privileged little ankle biter? You want me to order steak from room service?"

Mickey cleared his throat. "Wendy mashes the food with a fork."

"Oh my gods," Rachel muttered. She found a fork in a drawer and proceeded to pulverize the round pat in the bowl. "Wendy never wrote that in the instructions."

"Good thing I came with you," Mickey observed.

Rachel angled her head to find Mickey grinning at her. He was enjoying himself. A titillating tingle dropped like a high-speed elevator to her pelvis. *Good for a hungry dog, maybe*, she thought. *Not so good for my overactive libido.*

Mopette daintily lowered her snout to the dish. While the dog ate, Rachel moodily wondered why, of all the meltingly handsome Hollywood actors staying in the hotel that weekend, Mickey shook her insides like a James Bond martini.

A few minutes later, outside the hotel at last, Mopette yipped and tugged on the leash in the direction of the golf course.

"Ooooh, no. One bath today was plenty." Rachel marched awkwardly in Candy's ill-fitting spike heels across the parking lot, aiming for the manicured lawn in the blurry distance. The ornery little dog resisted the leash, her short nails scraping the pavement. "Hold on, Mopette. A little further and you can do your business on the cushy grass."

Mickey suddenly grabbed her forearm. "Stop for a sec."

"Mopette is desperate to pee. Tell me later." Wrenching her arm loose, Rachel continued onward, intent on keeping her balance on the asphalt surface. The sooner the dog finished her toilette, the sooner Mickey'd return to the party and leave her alone. His presence, compounded by nerves, discombobulated her insides. Walking on tiptoes in heels forced her hips to sway and set the camera pendant swinging. She cupped it to still the motion. The edge of the lawn swam into view only a few feet away.

Mopette erupted in a frenzy of yips. Rachel dragged her onward. "Relax, you spoiled baby. We're almost there."

A horrifying throaty growl rolled through the air like thunder. Rachel halted abruptly. Mopette squealed, pirouetted into a one-eighty, and scrambled in the opposite direction until yanked up off front legs by the leash. Rachel wobbled. Her free arm flailed in the air. Over Mopette's frantic yips, she heard Mickey say, "I tried to warn you!"

"Of what?"

"That German shepherd."

Ear-splitting ferocious barks swallowed Mopette's terrified protests. The little dog shot into the air on stubby legs like coiled springs. Rachel lunged to grab the animal before she crashed onto the hard pavement.

"It's attacking us!" Rachel tumbled into Mickey's arms, Mopette clutched in a football hold. "Save us, Mickey."

"Titan, quiet." Mercifully the beast obeyed an authoritative female voice and shut up. "Sorry to scare your cat, but you did approach us."

Rachel pulled her face off Mickey's white shirt, regained her balance, and wrapped both arms protectively around the quivering pet. "She's a Maltese *dog*. Who *are* you?"

"Catrina Turner, ma'am. Titan and I are on security patrol."

A dark-haired woman in a trim short-sleeved navy uniform emerged from the blurry background and closed the distance between them. A whine drifted on the evening air from a massive creature at her heels. Mickey sputtered, coughed, and cleared his throat.

Rachel glared at him over Mopette's soft fur pressed against her cheek. "How can you laugh? The poor thing is terrorized by that…that Cujo!" To the woman, she asserted, "This hotel doesn't have dog patrols."

Mickey placed a reassuring palm on Rachel's midback. "This weekend it does. Halden hired private security to keep out the paparazzi."

"Oh," Rachel said in a small voice. Then a sensation of warmth suffused her abdomen, and it wasn't a Mickey-triggered sexy flush. A dark stain spread from Mopette's butt down to the hem of Candy's sapphire silk dress. "Can this day get worse?" she wailed.

The security guard handed Mickey a business card. "Turner and Pooch Security at your service, sir. I'm a former cop, and Titan is a retired police service dog. We're patrolling the grounds this weekend."

Mickey flashed a smile guaranteed to charm the panties off any woman. "I'm Mickey McNichol, a groomsman. I'll report to Halden Armstrong that you're doing a great job. Let's hope your German shepherd scares the piss out of any paparazzi too." Mickey removed the comforting palm from Rachel's back, slid the card into the inside pocket of his jacket, and reached to shake the guard's hand.

Feeling abandoned, Rachel held fast to a wriggling dog hell-bent on escape. Titan raised his enormous snout and sniffed Mopette's scent like a dog checking out a tasty snack. The quivering ball of fluff buried a wet nose in Rachel's armpit and whimpered. On Mopette's behalf, she glared at the police dog the size of a miniature pony but a thousand times more lethal.

Wide-eyed, the attractive security guard in her early thirties grinned at Mickey, her grip locked over his hand tighter than handcuffs. "Pleased to meet you, sir," she said in a voice as sweet as a chocolate sundae.

Rachel gritted her teeth. Another lust-struck female. Rachel knew the signs better than anyone. He had the woman's card and her interest. He'd probably call and invite the guard to swing by his ground-floor room with the king bed for a shift report.

Mickey had every right to enjoy himself. In fact, the female distraction meant Rachel'd be out from under his eagle eye, free to take photos without being observed. Then why, with hours of picture-taking opportunities ahead, did she feel wretchedly abandoned?

Patience waning, Rachel interjected, "Mickey, the rehearsal dinner."

Mickey gave his hand a mild shake to encourage Catrina to release it.

Blinking, the guard remembered Rachel and stepped away. Her smile became professional. "Ma'am. Titan and I will be patrolling until Sunday evening. Until then, I suggest you avoid walking your toy dog near the perimeter of the hotel property." Titan's enthusiastic bark reinforced her advice.

"I'll do that," Rachel promised from the bottom of her heart.

The guard flicked the leash attached to Titan's harness, instructed the German shepherd to heel, and resumed their patrol.

Mopette, hardly larger than a rabbit, was of a size to fit inside that beast's massive jaw with room enough for her own forearm. Rachel blew out a breath at the narrow escape. Then a more pressing emergency trickled into her awareness.

She cursed under her breath. "I have to clean my dress."

"And I have to change as well."

Rachel wrenched her attention from the security team's retreating blurry forms to the red imprint of her very own lips on Mickey's white shirt, front and center between the jacket lapels.

"I may never wash this shirt," he smirked.

She cringed. "Ha-ha. Funny."

A sorry-looking pair in ruined outfits was how they appeared to late-arriving guests pulling up in an expensive vehicle. Rachel checked the time—seven-forty—and gasped. Twenty minutes until dinner. Candy had insisted that her "cousin" sit with the other bridesmaids. The maître d' had surely begun escorting guests to their seats. She absolutely needed a shower and to rinse the expensive silk dress. Unless heat from a blow-dryer might damage it? Otherwise she had absolutely *nothing* to wear.

With no other recourse, Rachel bit her bottom lip, gathered her courage, and for the first time in her life made a request of a guest instead of the other way round. "Can you do me a huge favor?"

"Sure." Mickey's amused expression gave her hope he wasn't angry that she'd soiled his shirt.

"After you change, please give Wendy a message? I'll be here for a couple of minutes so Mopette can do her business, but then I must meet Wendy in the Bridal Suite."

"No problem. Here's the doggy bag." He handed her the biodegradable bag he'd stowed in his trouser pocket. A bag she'd completely forgotten.

"Thank you." She took it and lowered Mopette to the grass. And waited.

Mickey hadn't moved. With arms crossed over his lipstick-stained white shirt, he watched Mopette sniffing the grass in the tight circle permitted by the leash. The tiny dog's quivering eased as Titan's scent dissipated in the breeze.

"You don't know much about dogs, do you?"

No harm in admitting the obvious, Rachel decided. "Not a thing."

"I've decided to add one more task to my groomsman duties."

"Oh?" Her spirits plummeted to her throbbing toes. She miserably assumed Mickey planned to rat out her incompetence to Candy and Halden. Head lowered, she dared to peek through lash extensions at his very determined expression, waited for him to ruin her future.

Then to her astonishment, he leaned in to press cool lips to one burning cheek. "I'm taking you and Mopette under my wing for the rest of the weekend."

Mouth agape, Rachel watched him stride in the direction of the hotel entrance. Then she clamped her lips closed to contain the dismayed *Arghhh* that surged up her throat. She fingered the pendant. Any other time she'd have been over the moon at the prospect of a hot chaperone.

How in the galaxy can I take photos with Mickey dogging my heels along with Mopette? And what if he sees me doing it?

Chapter 7

Hooked

"Dry-clean only." With a manicured forefinger Wendy flicked the tag on the pee-stained sapphire silk dress that Rachel had borrowed from Candy. "Do you own a semiformal outfit?"

Rachel, a towel wrapped around her body and damp from a brief shower, merely shivered in the air-conditioned Bridal Suite.

Wendy sighed. "From the expression on your face, I take it that's a no."

Mopette yipped enthusiastically from her perch on the cushioned vanity stool, a little princess on a plush throne. It was difficult to be upset with such a cutie, Rachel admitted. Mopette loved the company, she realized, and wondered how many hours a day the dog normally spent alone.

Wendy hurried into the walk-in closet jammed with a floor-length wedding gown, bridesmaids' dresses, shoes, and several suitcases' worth of women's clothing arranged on hangers.

"Where are Halden's clothes?" Rachel wondered aloud.

"They booked the room next door to use for his dressing room," came the muffled voice inside the closet. She extracted a silver-sequined long-sleeved dress. "Candy decided not to wear this little number this weekend because it's more summery here in Canada than she expected."

Rachel dropped the towel, took the sequined dress and stepped into it.

"Remove your bra," Wendy warned. "Can't you see it's backless? *Oh my god.* You're wearing granny panties? Candy wears a thong with that dress. Otherwise lines will show through the stretchy fabric."

Rachel obediently removed her underwear, folded the items, and piled them on top of the halter top, skirt, and flip-flops she'd left piled on the closet floor when changing into the sapphire silk before the wedding rehearsal that afternoon.

Then she carefully wiggled into the dress. To her dismay, chilled nipples peaked the metallic figure-hugging fabric. It covered her bare derrière with only a couple of inches to spare. The dress was meant for walking in, not sitting.

Wendy crossed her arms, head cocked assessingly. "Your hips are curvier than Candy's, and your torso slightly shorter. Fortunately the stretchy material compensates. What's with that ugly pendant?"

Rachel gulped and fisted it protectively. "It's my lucky charm."

Wendy sighed. "If I let you borrow some of Candy's jewelry, she'll fire me. As it is, I'm on probation. None of her PAs last longer than six months. Where are the black Christian Louboutins?" She scanned the carpet and spied them by the sofa. "Did Mopette pee on them, too? No matter. We're out of time." Wendy randomly grabbed a crystal perfume bottle from the array on the vanity and spritzed Candy's pricy red-soled heels.

Rachel thrust swollen, aching toes into them, longing fervently for her comfortable Walmart runners. Savvy little

Mopette understood what putting on shoes meant. She yipped happily, hopped down off the stool, and trotted over to the suite entrance.

Wendy inserted two fingers under Mopette's jeweled leather collar and held the door open. "Sorry, baby girl, you can't leave. Be a good dog. Rachel will walk you in a few hours." She turned to Rachel. "You have the suite access card?"

"Sure do." Rachel held out her left arm. A plastic card dangled from the coiled wristband next to her wristwatch.

Wendy scrunched her snub nose. "Tacky bracelet. We're late, or I'd dig out a clutch to put that in." In the hall Wendy ensured the lock caught, then turned brightly to Rachel. "It's showtime!"

"Lights, camera, action," Rachel weakly rejoined. She clutched the pendant and managed a nervous smile. Wendy had no idea that the "lucky charm" represented the key to her future career.

★★★★★

Mickey illuminated his phone screen to see the time. Tiffany sat to his left at the six-person round table reserved for the bridesmaids and groomsmen near the window overlooking the grounds. He had no quibble with the seating plan. In fact, he'd rearranged the name cards earlier to situate himself between the two women of interest to him.

But Tiffany was all about Tiffany at the best of times, and this was one of those times. She'd amped up sophisticated ingenue charm to make herself the center of attention, only to pout when male attention drifted away. Garth at her other side listened avidly to the story of her audition for the Bond-girl role. Mickey had witnessed the screen test and had heard the story a dozen times. Unfortunately, when Tiffany flipped "on," no one dared to interrupt the performance for fear of ruining her mood. She had a tendency to drink away irritation when ignored.

Mickey bided his time, waiting for an opening to remind her of his own role in snagging that crucial audition. He patted the inside pocket of his suit jacket, felt the contract, and shifted his shoulders impatiently. Ticktock.

Dinner service began. Busy servers filled crystal glasses with white wine and sparkling water, and served salads to the hundred guests. Candy, Halden, and their respective parents sat at a round table in the center of the spacious, chandelier-lit dining room.

Where is that girl?

Two women appeared at the entrance to the dining room, one tall and light, the other short and dark.

Rachel, at last. He raised an arm and waved. Candy's efficient assistant pointed at his table beside the window, then sidled sideways to an empty chair at a table adjacent to the kitchen entrance.

Rachel set out in his direction, her silver dress sparkling in reflected light from myriad crystal prisms dangling from overhead chandeliers. Her long-legged figure slowly wove between occupied chairs like a glistening trout swimming upstream. In her wake, the clink of glasses, cutlery, and dishes abruptly ceased. The servers froze in midaction, blatantly staring. Conversations died. Guests rubbernecked to see what or who had distracted the servers from their duties.

As Rachel carefully approached the vacant chair next to Mickey on those damnably treacherous heels, his gaze traveled from nipples budding the skintight fabric to a narrow waist, curvy hips, and sleek-muscled bare legs that went on forever. His thumping heart pulsed hot blood to his groin. He'd no idea that such a spectacular figure lurked under the straight dress she'd worn that afternoon.

His mouth opened to welcome her, but his brain had disconnected. For one of the very few times in his life, words escaped him. He identified with a trout hanging openmouthed off a fish fly—purely and simply hooked.

The men at the table pushed back their chairs and stood politely. Tiffany pursed artificially plumped lips and narrowed her heavily made-up eyes.

Rachel lay a slender hand on the back of the vacant chair. "Do I belong here?"

Mickey immediately pulled it out for her. "Yes, you belong to me. I, ah—I meant to say, you're beside me." His neck heated. On Rachel's other side, Wade arched his brows.

For decency's sake, Rachel held on to the hem of the microdress with both hands while she lowered her butt onto the chair. Searing pain from the blisters firing her heels finally eased. Fixated on every agonizing step across the room, she hadn't spared a thought to nervousness about being late. Or about angering Candy. Small mercies, because without her glasses, she hadn't a clue where in the room Candy and Halden sat.

Under the table, hidden by the white linen tablecloth, Rachel toed off the instruments of torture, exhaled with relief, and pressed bare skin against the chairback's cool fabric. She'd made it, no thanks to leaky Mopette.

A server moved swiftly to fill her glass with white wine. Oh, she longed to drown the butterflies in her stomach. But the challenges of the evening demanded sharp wits. Instead, the action of taking tiny sips conveniently masked scrutiny of the other bridesmaids.

At Mickey's other elbow, Tiffany's breasts begged for attention. Unnaturally oversized for the starlet's slight physique, the ripe globes mounded from a low-cut pink satin slip dress. A strand of blush pearls drew the observer's eye up the exquisite length of a creamy throat to the porcelain perfection of a classically beautiful face. Curled tendrils of hair artfully escaped from blond hair twisted into a chignon.

No wonder Asta, rather than exquisite Tiffany, had been elevated to maid of honor in the original's absence. By the bride's side in wedding photos, Tiffany's lush breasts would've certainly drawn every male's attention away from Candy's willowy figure. Rachel patted the camera pendant and thought about tabloid-worthy camera angles for photos of Tiffany.

Across the table, Asta lowered one eyelid in a languid wink acknowledging Rachel's perusal. Asta and Tiffany shared height and pale-blond hair color, but there the superficial resemblance ended. A chunky turquoise necklace accented Asta's turquoise linen tunic. The smart, unpretentious look complemented her athletic, tanned shoulders and muscled biceps. Dressing in wildly expensive shoes and revealing clothing wasn't at all comfortable. Asta apparently didn't feel pressure to compete with the other Hollywood women.

Her natural-blond hair gathered in a high ponytail, Asta had Halden's eyes, or rather, their mother's Nordic blue eyes. Freckles dusted a snub nose framed by high cheekbones curved in amusement. Rachel had thoroughly enjoyed chatting with her at the rehearsal cocktail event. Unfortunately the public wouldn't be interested in photos of Asta, who was definitely the friendlier of the other two bridesmaids.

Tiffany picked up her fork and the men followed her lead. Wade said in Rachel's right ear, "Relax and enjoy yourself. Have some more wine."

She stiffened, glancing left and right to find Mickey and Wade observing her. *Yikes.* She was so accustomed to being on the outside looking in that she'd completely forgotten to play her part in this show.

"You startle like a frightened bird every time someone speaks to you," Wade said. "Please believe me, we're fun once you get to know us."

Her stomach in knots, Rachel blurted without thinking, "I'll take that under advisement."

In the act of sipping his wine, Wade sputtered. "Are you a law student?"

Interested, they all paused and politely awaited her answer. *Beam me up, Scotty.* She wasn't prepared to converse with these sophisticated people so far out of her league.

Stupefied at finding herself the center of attention, Rachel filled the expectant silence with the truth. "I'm a huge fan of legal-drama television series."

Mickey set his water goblet on the table. "Hey, Rachel does remind me of Ally McBeal. Good call, Wade." Behind her chair, he and Wade fist-bumped.

"That dippy lawyer who sees an imaginary dancing baby?" Asta interjected from her seat beside Wade. "Guys, be nice." To Rachel she added, "Don't let the teasing bother you. They only rib girls they like."

Ally McBeal? Heat flamed her cheeks. She'd *loved* Calista Flockhart in that show, which she'd binge watched on Netflix the previous winter. When it first aired, she'd been a child. Mortified, Rachel bent over the salad, vowing to keep her troublesome mouth shut.

The camera pendant dangled between her breasts. With nowhere to hide it except in plain sight, she'd have to bide her time in order to take photos at the table under the noses of these sharp people. Or wait until they had too much to drink. Who knew taking photos could be *so* complicated? At least she'd managed to snap a few awesome celebrities at the rehearsal, and had successfully downloaded them to her laptop despite the drenching her camera had taken thanks to Mopette. The day hadn't been a total washout so far in that respect.

[♫ "I Really Like You"]

Then there was Mickey. Charming Mickey with chiseled features and steel-hard muscles rippling under velvet skin she'd lathered with sunscreen. She'd messed up with Mopette twice under his eagle eye. He must consider her a complete ditz. An Ally McBeal-caliber ditz. She bit her bottom lip unhappily. Unwelcomed attraction fizzed her insides, warring with heartfelt desire not to spend more time than necessary in his dangerously watchful presence.

Mickey lay down his fork, having made his salad disappear in four bites. She ruefully inspected her own small but artistically presented endive, pear, and Roquefort salad sprinkled with walnut crumbs. In a normal day, Rachel consumed carb-loaded meals to replace thousands of calories burned in a long, labor-intensive shift. That afternoon's light spa lunch and a shrimp on a skewer left her faint with hunger. She swiftly polished off the delicious salad, then squinted greedily at Tiffany's untouched plate.

"I admire a woman who enjoys food and doesn't mind showing it," Mickey murmured for her ears alone. "So many women at parties appear to survive on champagne and caviar."

Asta snagged one of the fresh-baked multigrain rolls from a silver basket and slathered it with a ball of iced butter. "Except Asta, of course," Mickey continued. "And now you." Cool fingers lightly tapped her bare thigh under the tablecloth.

At the delicious contact, Rachel's brain emptied of all coherent thought. She blurted the truth. "We're working women. I'd fade away to nothing if I ate like this every day." She indicated her empty plate.

Mickey angled to face her. "What is it that you do, exactly?"

Oh my gods. She'd blithely set herself up for that question. She slunk low in her chair, quavered, "Do?"

"Yeah," Wade said to the table at large. "What does Candy's cousin do in Toronto?"

The men's attention fastened on Rachel. Tiffany's green-eyed glare spit daggers.

Asta leaned forward, chin cupped in one palm. "Candy never mentioned you before today. But then Candy has been notoriously closemouthed about her own sister. Tell us about yourself."

Desperately stalling, Rachel licked a crumb of strong Roquefort blue cheese off her upper lip. That spring she'd completed a two-year community college Creative Photography program with top grades that garnered early acceptance into Toronto's prestigious, private film school for the fall semester. She'd supported herself while attending college with a part time minimum wage job as an evening room attendant in a three-star downtown hotel, and with summer jobs in the Muskoka resorts. Candy'd be furious if she revealed how she earned her living.

Nervy, Rachel twisted the cord holding her camera pendant. Her mother's rebuke in response to a childhood lie rang in her head: *It's not proper to hold back information, but it's a thousand times worse to lie on purpose.*

Rachel opted for the truth. "I've been accepted into Toronto Film School to study cinematography, starting in September. Wade, what do you do?"

Wade chuckled, apparently amused by her transparent attempt to deflect prying questions. Good natured, he played along. "I'm an entertainment attorney. Producers hire me to secure rights to a book or screenplay, negotiate equity financing deals, and vet distribution licenses for film projects. I have the satisfaction of helping independent films I believe in get green-lighted. No money, no movie."

"Do any Academy Awards decorate your mantle?"

He shook his head in exaggerated dismay. "Sadly, no. Producers get the screen credit." He threw out his hands, palms up. "I merely bask in the reflected glory."

Rachel decided she liked Wade's wry humor. She shifted her attention to Garth, ready to inquire about his profession, but Asta broke in.

"Rachel, you didn't answer Wade's question. What do you do *now*?"

Rachel stiffened. Her lips parted and resealed a couple of times—a fish out of water. She had nothing.

Mickey gallantly rescued her. "With a figure like Rachel's, I'd expect her cousin Candy paved the way to a modeling career in Canada."

Mickey knew full well a woman who hobbled in heels had no experience on a fashion runway. *So why cover for me?*

Garth, who'd kept his gaze fixed on Tiffany during the exchange, rumbled in his deep voice, "I like a woman who eats. Too many models starve themselves."

Tiffany, the former model, pouted Botoxed lips and pushed away her untouched salad. "Some of us have no choice."

A server whisked away the salad plates, replacing them with the main course. Now this was more like it: a rosy-fleshed grilled trout spanned the gilt-edged dinner plate between sides of miniature red, purple, and white roasted potatoes and long green beans sprinkled with slivers of almonds. With contented grunts, the men tucked in.

"Halden chose the rehearsal dinner entrée specifically for his Wisconsin fishing bros," Asta revealed to the table. "Enjoy the meal tonight, guys, because Candy selected the wedding banquet menu. You know what that means."

"Vegetarian?" Wade ventured. The men exchanged looks of horror.

Garth raised his fork to attract their attention. "Settle down. Halden promised to have wings and burgers available in the bar lounge. We'll sneak out after the speeches for some real food."

"As long as they're not soy burgers," Wade said darkly.

Relieved to be out of the spotlight, Rachel speared a miniature purple potato. Hollywood types appeared to be obsessed with food—the men with eating quantities of protein, and the women, excluding Asta, with *not* eating.

When the dinner plates, polished clean except for Tiffany's, were removed and replaced with empty dessert plates, the server set a platter of bite-sized *petits fours* in pastel shades of yellow, pink, lavender, and spring green in the center of the table.

"Where's your dessert?" Garth joked to the others.

Mickey picked up silver serving tongs and smiled at Rachel. "Preference?"

"I'll take two, please." She indicated a pink one-inch cube topped with a blue forget-me-not flower made of frosting, and a pale green cube adorned with a mint leaf.

He placed her choices on her plate, and a yellow cube on Tiffany's plate. A mere formality because Tiffany ignored it.

When all were served, Rachel delicately bit through a coat of brittle pink icing to featherlight layers of cake and creamy filling that dissolved on her tongue in a burst of almond, buttercream, and sugary flavors.

Heavenly. As a child she'd pressed her nose to glass cases in the bakery and dreamed that someday she'd eat as many confections as her tummy'd hold. Tonight they were hers for the asking at a fancy dinner seated between two equally drool-worthy, delectable movers and shakers from Hollywood. She pinched the back of her hand, unable to believe her luck.

Their server offered tea and coffee. Rachel requested a double espresso for the jolt of caffeine. She examined her wristwatch under the table—almost ten. The opportunity to take photos in the dining room was running out like sand in an egg timer.

Candy and Halden approached their table. Candy's friend Raynald trailed in their wake, his digital SLR capturing a stream of photos of the couple and their guests.

"We're circulating, darlings," Candy announced gaily. Then she noticed Rachel attired in *her* silver-sequined dress. The hundred-watt smile dimmed to twenty-five. *Oh-oh.* Candy's topaz eyes flashed cold annoyance.

Asta broke in before the strain ruptured into an outburst. "Candy, dear, please show us your fabulous diamond. It's breathtaking." Distracted, Candy gracefully extended her slender white arm to allow all to admire the sparkling gem. Raynald snapped shots from various angles.

Whew. Saved by a $50,000 brilliant-cut diamond.

At his bride-to-be's side, Halden's head brushed a low-hanging crystal suspended from the overhead chandelier. Light bounced off hundreds of glittering chandelier crystals, haloing Halden and Candy's glamorous blond figures in shards of radiant light. From Rachel's seated angle, the light created a dazzling backdrop better than effects in a portrait studio. While the others at the table made appropriate laudatory comments to their hosts about the meal and the guests, Rachel rapidly aimed the hidden camera and pressed the noiseless shutter button.

Candy touched Halden's elbow to signal the transition to the next table. Her intended hastened to inform the groomsmen of his plans for their entertainment. "I've ordered Cuban cigars and thirty-year-old Scotch whisky in the screened Muskoka Room at eleven. I'll join you there after Candy retires to get her beauty sleep." He gazed adoringly down at her with puppy-dog eyes. "Although I can't imagine how Candy can possibly be any more beautiful tomorrow than she is tonight."

The men quickly murmured agreement. Tiffany twitched her flat butt in her chair and reached for the wine glass she'd ordered refilled when offered tea. In one motion Garth deftly swiped the glass from under her hand and placed it on the tray of a passing server. For a muscle-bound giant, he moved like the Flash.

Garth ignored Tiffany's peeved pout. "Does Candy have plans for the ladies?"

"Careful, Tiff, darling. Forehead lines, remember?" Asta stage-whispered. Louder she said, "Candy needs her beauty sleep. Didn't you hear?"

Garth pushed to his feet. "In that case, Tiffany, would you care to join me for a stroll along the beach?"

Tiffany looked up at him from under long artificial lashes, an internal struggle evident for all to see on her expressive face. "Perhaps the gentlemen would prefer to join me in the bar for a nightcap before I retire?"

Wade shook his head. "Sorry, Tiff. Jet lag. I plan to catch forty winks until Halden joins us later."

The table broke up. Tiffany stood, swaying slightly, breasts protruding like two pink cantaloupes on a swizzle stick. Rachel watched her with concern. The actress had consumed a few bites of fish and the green beans—certainly not enough food in her stomach to soak up several glasses of white wine.

Despite the double espresso, fatigue leadened Rachel's limbs. It had been a long day. After she swung by the Bridal Suite to return the dress and shoes and walk little Mopette, she'd have plenty of time to download the photos and read her email before collapsing into bed.

Earlier she'd fired off emails to a couple of photo agencies to query whether they were interested in buying celebrity images from an unknown freelancer. The photo agencies in turn sold the images to tabloids, entertainment news television shows, and websites.

First Rachel needed to retrieve the heels she'd toed off. She stretched out one throbbing foot to feel around under the table for the instruments of torture.

"Searching for these?" Mickey kicked the shoes over to his reaching hand, then lifted them to her lap.

"Thank you." Embarrassment heated her skin. "My feet are killing me."

"I guessed as much. Allow me to massage them," he invited in a suggestive tone for her ears only. "We'll go somewhere private."

Like his room. "Ah—" Her cheeks burned. Her female anatomy shouted *do it*! But she had important things to accomplish that evening. Things that unfortunately did not involve Mickey rubbing her body parts. "Can I take a rain check?" Sincere regret softened the rejection. "I'm due to walk Mopette one last time this evening."

"Then I'll join you. I have an hour to kill before the men gather for Halden's bachelor party. I'll enjoy the fresh air." He grinned at her consternation. "And your company, of course."

Chapter 8

Splash

Barefoot, with Candy's designer shoes tucked under one arm, Rachel inserted the master key card dangling from her wrist into the Bridal Suite lock and pushed open the door. A sleepy Mopette trotted over from her cushy makeshift bed—the satin cushion she'd pulled off the vanity stool. Rachel automatically stooped to pick up the cushion and fluff it before replacing it on the stool. The dog yipped a greeting and sniffed Rachel's raw, swollen toes.

Bedside lamps glowed in the adjacent bedroom. Mopette trailed Rachel as she padded on throbbing feet through to the bathroom to ensure it had been freshened satisfactorily for the guests' return. She switched on the bathroom light. Porcelain fixtures gleamed. Clean towels, robes, and bathmat? Check. Dry shower curtain? Check. New soap and toiletries? Check. On her return trip, she verified that the night attendant had placed a chocolate in foil on each night table and turned down the king comforter at a precise angle. The guests expected five-star service, and they got it.

To her dismay, Mickey had insisted he'd wait for her and Mopette on the dining room terrace, in line with the unwelcomed promise earlier that he planned to "take them under his wing," code for "watch her every move." Guilt nipped at her blistered heels. Or was that Mopette's rough pink tongue? She picked up the dog and rubbed her nose in warm, soft fur. Mopette arched to lick Rachel's ear.

At this point in an exhausting day, she didn't have energy left to fend off suspicious, probing questions. But the show must go on. Resigned to the inevitable, she planned to give the dog the shortest walk in history and then escape to her room to download the photos.

After lowering Mopette onto the cushioned stool, Rachel quickly stripped off Candy's dress and hung it safely in the walk-in closet. She wiped down the designer shoes with a damp tissue and placed them alongside a dozen pairs worth more than a year's minimum wage income. Then, stark naked except for the camera pendant, skin goose-bumped by chilly air-conditioning, she turned to where she'd left the halter top, skirt, and underwear on the floor in a corner of the closet.

No clothes.

Only her black flip-flops remained. Rachel dashed into the salon and cast about wildly. Every surface had already been tidied by the evening room attendant. The bright yellow color of a laundry claim ticket on the console by the door snagged her attention. *Oh my gods*!

"Mopette," she squealed. "Please don't tell me the night maid took my clothes to the laundry for overnight service. Tell me you've been a bad dog and dragged my clothes somewhere."

Rachel limped into the closet, around the bed, even onto the balcony. To Mopette, Rachel's frantic search was a game of chase. She barked enthusiastically at Rachel's heels. Thankfully, the Bridal Suite's isolated location at the end of the corridor on the inn's top floor prevented noise from disturbing other guests.

Ticktock. Candy'd return any minute. She wrung her hands, frantically considered the limited options. A bath towel wrapped sarong style would require her to detour to her own room to change. And besides, her own scruffy clothes would surely tip off Mickey to her fake bridesmaid's gig. Candy's silver designer dress beckoned from the closet, but Rachel shuddered at the memory of Candy's flash of anger when she recognized the dress earlier at dinner. No more borrowing, then.

Two white cotton robes hung behind the bathroom door, sleeves tucked into pockets embroidered with the Sterling Inn logo: one size small, the other extra large. In a hotel robe and flip-flops, she'd easily pass for a guest.

Counting on the tradition that Halden would sleep in the room adjacent to the suite the night before his wedding, Rachel slid the oversized robe meant for him off its hanger. She thrust arms into sleeves longer than the tips of her fingers, wrapped the long belt twice around her waist and knotted it, and then scampered into the salon to retrieve her flip-flops and Mopette's leash.

Clutching Mopette tight to her thumping heart, Rachel heard the elevator door ding as they exited the self-locking suite. An unintelligible comment in Candy's trilling voice and Raynald's fawning reply drifted down the hall. *Yikes.* Rachel pinned Mopette's nose and jaw together to stifle her greeting to her mistress, slammed open the heavy fire door to the stairwell, and plunged down the stairs.

★★★★★

In his bathroom Mickey brushed his teeth, combed his hair, and swiped a palm across his jawline. Yup, his five o'clock shadow merited a quick shave to protect Rachel's sensitive skin. He loosened his tie and lathered up.

Awareness of the unsigned contract tucked in the inside breast pocket of his bespoke Italian suit jacket overshadowed his anticipation of private time with Rachel.

With Monday's nonnegotiable deadline to sign the commercial property lease, pressure to add an up-and-coming star, or preferably two, to his roster of clients ratcheted higher with every passing hour. Commissions from his film crew and aspiring screenwriter clients didn't generate sufficient revenue to cover the expense of prime office space for his new agency. Delonda, his indispensable executive assistant, believed in him and had agreed to quit her job at Herron Talent Agency and follow him to his new agency, provided he lined up enough new clients to pay her salary and the bills.

Reentering the bedroom scant minutes later, he tossed the tie onto the bed. A glance at the bedside clock confirmed that he'd better hurry to intercept nearsighted Rachel before she ventured into the dark grounds with Mopette. Candy insisted on taking the dog everywhere, including across the US-Canada border. *The paperwork must have been a bitch.*

Although the warm evening didn't merit a jacket, keeping the contract close at hand did. He slid his smartphone into the front pocket of his trousers. In less than forty-eight hours Tiffany'd be back in the clutches of her conniving California manager, beyond his reach. With Garth attached to Tiff that weekend like an offensive tackle protecting his quarterback, Mickey aimed to convince him at the bachelor party that signing Tiffany to Mickey's new agency was in her best interest.

Everyone in Hollywood knew Halden's company produced three blockbuster films in five short years with Garth

Armstrong, chief operating officer, holding the production company reins. Renowned as the Man with the Midas Touch, Garth had one inexplicable blind spot: Tiffany.

When sober, Tiffany habitually took calculated actions that furthered her career, including her now-floundering marriage to an award-winning director that had generated a starring role. Widely considered a stunning filly bursting with talent, she appeared to be heading off the track to stardom unless, well…unless someone who put Tiffany's career first and foremost reined in Tiff's drinking. If not himself as Tiffany's handler, then Mickey had to acknowledge her career would benefit by adding Garth to her team.

Thus prepared for his date with Candy's amusing cousin and the bachelor party to follow, Mickey exited through his room's sliding doors, vaulted the low stone wall, and strolled across the lawn to the hotel's flagstone terrace to wait for Rachel-of-the-endless-legs.

A couple of dozen guests mingled, relaxed in Muskoka chairs, sipped nightcaps, and murmured conversationally in the cooling night air. Flickering flames of citronella torches kept mosquitoes at bay. A server shuttled back and forth to the bar inside with a tray laden with brandies and glass mugs of spiked coffee. Mickey shoved his hands in his trouser pockets and paced the length of the terrace.

Rachel. The pretty woman's naïve persona coupled with an uncanny gift for getting into trouble with Mopette kept him captivated. And chuckling.

To survive in his business, a talent agent needed to be astute about people—their characters, what they wanted, what drove them, how far they might go in the entertainment industry. Few had what it took to join the elite cadre of actors, directors, cinematographers, production designers, and other top talent. Agents rarely backed a dark horse. The better the odds of their clients' successes, the greater the commission revenue. Business was business. No successful agent afforded the luxury of marketing a dud.

Cutthroat competition to be signed by a top talent agent turned many ambitious men and women aggressive, manipulative, even desperate. He'd encountered several who were willing to cross an ethical line for a leg up in the industry. Mickey had been fooled by more than his share of falsely affectionate women until the inevitable bleak reality check. In contrast, Candy's unsophisticated cousin trembled at his touch yet attempted to keep her distance. A refreshing challenge.

Blurry movement in the deep gloom under the pines beyond the terrace caught his eye. A ghostly wraith drifted between trees. A white ball appeared to roll at lawn level.

He inhaled sharply. *Holy Hotel California*. He held his breath as the creepy forms advanced to twenty feet from the terrace and halted at the limits of the flickering torchlight. *Where are the Ghostbusters when you need them?*

"Mickey," the taller phantom hissed, beckoning with an undulating wave of an unearthly arm. "Over here."

"No thanks," he demurred. "It's not my time yet."

"Mickey!"

He cautiously stepped off the flagstones onto the grass. "Who or what in hell *are* you?"

In a loud whisper laced with urgency, the taller figure entreated, "It's me, Rachel. Hurry up. I don't want anyone to see us."

"Rachel? Why didn't you say so." He swiftly crossed the dew-damp lawn and entered the moonless gloom where Rachel waited, garbed in white from neck to ankles. With her blond hair, no wonder he'd mistaken her for a ghost from a distance.

Mopette sprung upright on her back legs, waved short front paws in the air, and yapped in greeting. "She's feisty for this time of night. What in the name of the afterlife are you wearing?"

"Please, Mickey. Keep your voice down. When we get far enough away from the guests, I'll explain." Rachel turned her back on him and unerringly wove between the trees on a heading for the lake, pulling a reluctant Mopette on the leash behind her.

Mickey swatted at the mosquito snacking on his neck. "I asked for this," he complained to no one in particular.

When their feet sank into sand at the water's edge, Rachel stopped. Mopette's ears perked high. Her body shook with excitement. Despite the late hour, she seemed to have gained a second wind. Yipping a demand to be allowed to advance, she strained on the end of the leash, nose pointed at the water.

"Oh no, you don't. One bath today was enough." Rachel slapped a mosquito burrowing its stinger into one cheek. "The bugs sure are vicious tonight."

"Let's try the dock," Mickey urged with an outstretched hand. "The night breeze off the cooling lake discourages mosquitoes."

Rachel accepted his grasp. They walked hand in hand the length of the long wood-plank dock to a wide platform where, during the day, white wooden Muskoka chairs provided lounging guests with an unobstructed view the length of the lake. Soothing sounds of chirping cicadas, Mopette's snuffles, and water lapping at the wooden structure drained the tensions of the day. Overhead millions of pinpricks of light in an inky blanket cocooned them in a private universe.

"I've only seen stars like this in Wisconsin," he said.

"On your fishing trips?"

"That's right. Of course, I was with the guys. Tonight I'm with you."

At his side, her strong, slender fingers entwined in his, Rachel's pale skin reflected starlight. Even enveloped in the preposterously oversized robe, her lean figure radiated unconscious sensuality. It'd been months, maybe a year, since he'd felt so attracted to a woman. Her enticing lips tempted him beyond a man's endurance. He angled his head to press his mouth against hers.

Rachel released his hand, retreated a couple of steps to duck his kiss, and pulled Mopette on a short leash with her. "Mickey," she began. Mopette deked around her in an attempt to sniff the water, wrapping the leash around her legs in the process.

Given the signals she'd been sending, Mickey wondered at Rachel's withdrawal. She hadn't brushed away his hand on her thigh under the dinner table. On the contrary she'd seemed to enjoy it. An obvious explanation occurred to him. His gut clenched. He never knowingly poached another man's woman. "Do you have a boyfriend?"

"No," she admitted. "But I can't get involved with a guest—I mean to say…a wedding guest. At least not in public."

He dismissed the weak excuse, imagining she'd taste finer than the Scotch waiting for him in the Muskoka Room. "One kiss under the stars, Rachel. You're attracted to me. I know women."

"It's not that I don't *want* to kiss you, Mickey, truly, but someone might see us." She glanced nervously in the direction of the third-floor Bridal Suite windows, their curtains open, the illuminated interior a searchlight slicing the darkness.

Mickey advanced to close the distance between them. "We're two hundred feet from the hotel. No one will recognize us."

Rachel retreated. "We absolutely *cannot* fool around out here," she squeaked. "Seriously. Mopette needs to do her business and return to Candy. She'll be waiting." She lifted her face to the starry sky. A whisper of a regretful sigh escaped. "Although it *is* romantic."

Mickey took that as a yes. He advanced another step. At the same instant Mopette tugged on the leash. Rachel teetered on the edge of the dock, then plummeted backward into thin air with a shriek. She body-slammed the water with a splash loud enough to wake the dead. Mopette catapulted airborne at the end of the leash, her surprised yelp and splash an echo.

Mickey rushed to the edge of the dock. "Rachel!"

Her head broke the surface, wet hair gleaming dully, arms thrashing. Mopette paddled at full throttle nearby, too busy to yap.

"Save the dog!" Rachel coughed. Chilling gasps pierced the night air before the heavy weight of the sodden robe dragged her down into the black depths.

To hell with the dog. Mickey leaped off the dock, landing leather-shoe-shod feetfirst into cool water next to the last spot she'd surfaced. He filled his lungs, dove deep, and swung his arms in blind searching arcs. Precious seconds slipped by until frantic fingers penetrated a forest of slimy weeds rising from the bottom of the lake and encountered cotton. He fisted the fabric and, kicking with adrenaline-fueled energy, lunged for the surface.

Rachel's head bobbed above the surface for the second time. She sputtered, hacked up water, and sucked in air. Relief along with welcomed oxygen flooded his aching lungs. He inserted arms under her shoulders and clutched her heaving chest to his, thereby supporting her head and shoulders above water. Heart pounding, his legs scissored like strokes of an engine. He'd never been so scared in his life.

The wet robe, as heavy as a cement overcoat, threatened to force them both down into a watery grave.

"The robe has to go." As she gasped for air, he fumbled for the belt knot, loosened it with frantic fingers, and managed with difficulty to strip off the deadly soaked fabric. Under it, his hands encountered nothing but wet skin.

She was naked.

Chapter 9

What Happens in Muskoka Stays in Muskoka

Mickey's jaw sagged open, filling his mouth instantly with lake water. He spit it out, then wrapped an arm tighter around Rachel's buck-naked torso. "I've got you."

Breasts flattened against his ruined formal shirt as Rachel inhaled several deep lungfuls of air, coughed, and with a trembling hand pushed away wet hair covering her eyes.

"I'm okay now. I can swim." To prove it, she extended her arms to vigorously paddle to help keep them afloat. "Rescue Mopette!"

Over her shoulder Mickey scanned the inky lake surface for signs of white fur until he spied the small animal earnestly paddling toward the beach. "The mutt's fine."

She twitched her shoulders to loosen his grip. "Seriously, Mick. I can swim. Let me go."

"Not a chance," he growled, an attempt to mask ball-squeezing fear at the close call. "You almost drowned. No way I'm letting you go."

With legs weighed down by waterlogged wool trousers, he kicked toward shore, one arm supporting Rachel in a lifeguard hold. When his feet found the sandy lake bottom, and she was able to stand on tiptoe, he wrapped his other arm around her body and hugged her tight.

"You're naked." He stated the obvious.

Rachel hacked up more lake water. Her ribcage heaved with gasping lungfuls of air, her small firm breasts rhythmically rubbing against his wet shirt.

He'd almost lost her. The hundred pound robe had weighed her down like an anchor. Remnants of panic accelerated his heartbeat. He slid his hands down her back to cup her buttocks, squeezing the slick torso against the length of his as if afraid to let go. The pace of her pounding heart against his chest slowed. Easier breaths fanned his wet face.

As he relaxed, he became aware of the sound of Mopette's insistent, worried yips. He craned his neck to locate the source. A white blur scrabbled back and forth on the beach, splashed into shallow water in their direction, retreated, and repeated the pattern. Then the slippery woman shifted in his arms, and everything faded from his awareness except her.

"My hero." Rachel planted her mouth on his in a too-brief smooch. "That's for rescuing me."

[♫ "Love Came for Me"]

When he groaned a protest at her withdrawal, she wrapped her arms around his neck, hitched her body higher until her sweet center crested his dick, long legs scissoring his thighs. "This one is because I've been desperate to kiss you since the moment we met."

With better access to his mouth, an agile tongue tasted his, then teased his lips before plunging practically to his tonsils. She sucked his tongue with staggering passion. He fought to remain upright. His dick sprang to life despite the cool water, despite the scare.

Earlier that evening he'd watched Rachel approach the dinner table in that skin-hugging silver dress, his member straining against his zipper, his thoughts consumed with strategizing how to get Rachel *out* of that dress. He spared a second to fervently thank the universe for benevolently granting his wish before wrenching his mouth from her fierce lip-lock.

At her protesting whimper, he kissed her long throat in apology, kissed delicate collarbones, rained kisses down her chest on a trajectory to one of the pointed, firm breasts that so distracted him that not for a million bucks could he recall what he ate for dinner.

He nosed aside the pendant she wore everywhere to explore a nipple with his tongue. Rachel arched in the circle of his arms, thrusting her breasts above water level to give him unrestricted access. Throaty moans and pressure on the back of his head encouraged him to continue. Her entire body vibrated with mounting tension. He wanted a free hand to caress the sensitive bud grinding into his pelvis above his throbbing dick. He wanted to give her the release her body craved.

Most of all, he wanted a bed.

When he raised his nose to replenish his oxygen supply, Rachel gripped the back of his neck, guided his mouth to the other nipple. "Don't stop," she ordered in a fervent whisper. "This may be our only chance to be together this weekend."

He was confounded—release her so he could strip, or hold on. He decided to maintain a possessive grip on her slippery skin. *A bird in the hand, and all that.* "I can't make love to you in my clothes."

She placed a forefinger over his lips. "Shhh. Keep your voice down. Sound travels over water."

"It's a bit late to worry about—"

Rachel didn't let him finish. She planted her mouth on his and vacuumed his lips in another passionate, loin-stirring kiss. Her arms wrapped around his head and held him clamped to her in a vice grip. He was being ravished, he realized, not the other way around. This woman wanted him bad.

When she finally let him come up for air, he croaked, "My room."

"It's the only option," she agreed, chest heaving, breathing hard. "I need…I need—"

"Me?"

"I need another robe. Fortunately your room is on the ground floor. You can sneak in through the patio doors and then return to the lake with a robe for me."

Incredulous, he blurted, "You're planning to hide here in the lake? Come to my room, and we'll, ah, take care of the situation." The situation causing him the most discomfort at the moment was the painful erection in his sopping pants. One-track mind. He admitted it. He'd prefer to keep Rachel naked, at least for a couple of hours.

"Exterior security cameras," she warned.

"Ah, got it." *Damn.* Halden had arranged enough hotel security for a G20 Summit. No chasing a bare-ass beauty across the lawn tonight, then. His shoulders sagged in disappointment. Then a thought penetrated the rampant desire clouding his brain. "How do you know where my room is?"

"Um, I, ah, saw you leave it," Rachel replied.

"When exactly?" He jabbed the side of his head with the heel of his palm to dislodge water in his ears.

"Oh, earlier today." She released arms clutching his neck and slid down his front until perched on her toes on the lake bottom. "Seriously, Mickey. Someone from the hotel may show up any minute to investigate why Mopette is making such a racket." Her shoulders shivered in the cooling night air.

He sighed, resigned to the inevitable. "Right." He reluctantly released her and began trudging ashore. He'd put three feet between them when Rachel smacked a hand wetly to her forehead.

"Oh my gods. I just remembered. What if that monster dog is patrolling the grounds?" A pale arm extended in the direction of Mopette's yips on shore. "You'd better take Mopette with you."

"Right." Mickey sloshed beachward while brainstorming an alternate scenario, preferably one that involved getting rid of the dog and lathering Rachel under a hot shower.

Eventually he reached the sandy beach. Water streamed from his weighty jacket and trousers. The dry-clean only, 100 percent wool suit must've absorbed at least thirty pounds of water. He sighed, suddenly bone tired.

"What's wrong?" Rachel called from where she'd retreated to conceal herself neck deep in water. "Are you all right?"

"Just wondering if wool shrinks."

Mopette trotted up to him and pawed his leg in greeting. Then the bedraggled critter shook like a rattle, peppering his trousers with the sand she'd rolled in. Heaving another heavy sigh, Mickey bent to pick up the dog's trailing leash. Unlike his ruined $2,000 suit, Mopette didn't appear to be any the worse for wear. Her jeweled pink bow, on the other hand, gleamed on the sand. He snagged it and stuffed it in his empty trouser pocket.

"Give me ten minutes," he called to Rachel. Starlight illuminated the dark blob of her head emerging from the lake surface like the Loch Ness monster. "I'll be back," he growled in his best imitation of Arnold Schwarzenegger.

Gratified by the soft snicker echoing across the water, he squelched in grit-filled leather shoes across sand to the granite steps rising to the upper lawn. The tired dog slowed, and he bent to pick her up.

A thought penetrated pleasurable plans for what he'd do to Rachel when he eventually enticed her into a bed. The guys in the Muskoka Room were probably wondering what kept him. Automatically he reached into his trouser pocket for his phone. His fingers closed around Mopette's bow. He shifted the dog and rammed a hand into the other pocket. Empty. The smartphone loaded with important contacts that were the livelihood of an agent apparently rested on the bottom of the lake, sacrificed to Rachel's rescue.

Dammit. However, no big deal. He always backed up his contact list in the cloud.

Then a tsunami of alarm washed away irritation. The draft contract! He patted the suit jacket inner pocket.

Dammit to hell! The sheaf of paper crucial to his future was a sodden ruin.

Chapter 10

You've Got Email

Mopette sat obediently in a spa salon chair admiring herself in the mirror, enjoying the stream of warm air from Marie-Eve's blow-dryer rippling damp white fur.

"Obviously the princess's pet is accustomed to this treatment," Rachel groused. "Unlike me." Between passes she aimed the handheld dryer at the camera pendant dangling from her neck between the folds of the robe Mickey had retrieved from his room. A big fat tear plopped onto Mopette's fur.

The expensive secret camera had come with a manufacturer's warning to keep the delicate mechanism away from high heat and moisture. Lake Muskoka was moist. It was beyond moist.

When Mickey arrived back at the lake dressed in running shorts and a T-shirt and with a tired Mopette wrapped in a robe under one arm in a football carry, Rachel had urged Mickey to join his friends in the screened Muskoka Room.

"I have to bathe and return Mopette before she's missed," Rachel had insisted on the beach, gratefully accepting the proffered robe to cover her dripping nakedness. "I know you'd prefer another, uh, activity," she'd acknowledged, sensing his smoking gaze hot enough to evaporate the droplets on her skin. "So would I, to be frank." When he'd leaned in to steal another kiss, she dodged to one side and relieved him of Mopette instead. "Duty calls."

She neglected to add that, after returning Mopette safely to the Bridal Suite, she had an even more urgent task: to find out if the pictures she'd snapped at the rehearsal dinner had survived the prolonged dunking.

The stream of warm air from the dryer nozzle soothed Mopette. Her eyelids drooped. Sleepily she circled on the salon chair, preparing to curl up for a snooze.

Rachel fluffed the soft fur at the scruff of the dog's neck, checking for dampness and stray particles of sand. "All dry, sweetie," she said, surprising herself. What was this sweetie talk? The little scamp was growing on her. She released an exhausted sigh.

They'd both survived an emotionally draining day. For Mopette, Titan had probably scared her out of two years' growth. For Rachel, when Mickey kissed her in the lake, her uninhibited response in retrospect both exhilarated and alarmed her.

Fantasizing about an unattainable guest was safe.

Drooling over a Hollywood hunk from afar was safe.

Actually kissing him felt far from safe. If not for that suit he wore, things could have gotten out of hand. Or rather in her hand. Or in her.

The terrifying reality was that she lusted after Mickey like no man in her entire twenty-two years. And the distraction of wanting to be with him, touch him, hang on his every word and facial expression, at a time when her future career relied on keeping her focus, literally, on the bride and groom? *Not* good.

She disconnected the blow-dryer and returned it to Marie-Eve's station. "Sorry, Mopette. You can't sleep here in the spa." Rachel scooped the dog, limp and cuddly as a plush toy, into her arms.

After quietly cracking open the Bridal Suite door wide enough to nudge Mopette inside, Rachel dashed through empty corridors and stairwells to her small room in the staff quarters above the laundry. Cross-legged on the single bed at last, she booted her laptop and glanced at her alarm clock. Midnight.

The moment she'd been dreading since her backside smacked the surface of Lake Muskoka had arrived. She attached one end of a cable to the laptop and the other to the slot in the miniature camera encased in the pendant, praying with all her heart while waiting for the folder with contents of the camera files to open on the screen.

The file didn't open. Damaged chip.

The bottom dropped out of her world. *Worst-case* scenario. No hidden camera for wedding photos! The cocktail event and rehearsal dinner photos of Candy flashing her bling might be retrievable by an expert, but she didn't have the luxury of time. Besides, the entertainment media paid for scoops, not yesterday's news.

She accessed her email account and clicked on a single reply from a photo agency. With mounting excitement, she scanned the offer to buy Kane-Armstrong wedding photos for $20,000 as long as the quality was acceptable, the agency obtained exclusive rights, and she uploaded them to the agency server within an hour of the Saturday afternoon wedding.

Both hands flew to her mouth. *Twenty thousand dollars!*

Then cruel reality swamped premature elation. She had a buyer but no hidden camera. No camera, no photos.

Supremely frustrated, she flung herself sideways on the bed. Bitter tears trickled onto the polyester bedspread. *The gods want me to abandon the dream of becoming a Hollywood camera operator. Why else make taking pictures so difficult?*

Yet her mother hadn't raised a quitter. Rachel reached for a tissue, blew her nose, and pushed herself to sitting position. In one palm she bounced the water-damaged camera pendant that she'd pinned her dreams on. Where to obtain a replacement?

Muskoka cottage country shoppers ordered specialty items online or drove two hours to Toronto. Buying another miniature camera before the afternoon wedding wasn't a realistic option. Neither was the bulky professional digital SLR purchased for her college courses.

The smartphone charging on the nightstand dinged with a notification. She snatched it up. An older silver-colored 3G model, it captured photos and video. Then an idea occurred to her. *Attach it to the flower stems with elastic bands deep inside the bouquet, separate the flowers for an unobstructed view, and voilà: a hidden camera.*

She activated silent mode, plugged it into the charger, and patted it for good luck. "Hey, phone, you're my only hope."

★★★★★

Rachel's alarm clock buzzed at seven o'clock on Saturday morning. After a quick shower in the communal staff bathroom, she flipped open her laptop and logged into her inbox to find a new email from the Toronto Film School, but nothing from another agency interested in buying the Kane-Armstrong wedding photos. So no bidding war then.

She clicked on the email, a reminder from Admissions warning students that failure to pay a substantial tuition deposit by July 15 would result in withdrawal of acceptance into the program. Rachel winced. *More pressure is just what I need on the day of the wedding.*

Next she pulled up Wendy's daily schedule on her fully charged phone. After Mopette's morning walk, Rachel was expected to join the wedding party and guests between nine and eleven for a poolside buffet breakfast. Dress code: swimsuits.

Her photographer side bounced with excitement. *Dozens of beautiful stars arrayed mostly naked around the pool. Fantastic photo op!*

She rooted through a drawer for the lost and found bikini, and dangled the cracker-sized leopard-print triangles by the attached strings. Her socks contained more material! On her body, the bikini scarcely covered her nipples and crotch. Her reflection in the mirror flushed crimson. The sheer cover-up, practical only because it had a pocket for her phone, and flip-flops completed the outfit.

Chill, she psyched her embarrassed reflection. *No one will be watching a nobody like you at the pool. Not with all those gorgeous movie stars around.*

The staff will get an eyeful of you, her inner voice challenged. *You've gotta live that down for the rest of the summer.*

I'll never see any of the staff again after I start film school. This photo op is too awesome to pass up!

On her way to pick up Mopette in the Bridal Suite, Rachel surrendered to a growling stomach and popped into the staff dining room to grab a cup of coffee and a toasted bagel.

While Rachel ate, a gossipy kitchen cook gleefully relayed employee reactions to Rachel's bridesmaid charade.

They ranged from leering comments (male) to envy (female) to her supervisor Angeline's dire prediction that Rachel'd be banished to the hot-as-Hades laundry when the GM caught sight of her. Juanita, the stacked front desk agent, had complained to anyone who'd listen that *she,* not a plain string bean, deserved to have been selected to replace the missing bridesmaid.

Plain string bean, eh? Rachel swallowed the last bite of a bagel slathered with cream cheese on the way to the Bridal Suite. Mickey didn't seem repelled by her twiggy limbs and microbreasts. Core tingling, she recalled exhilarating sensations of seeking hands gliding over bare skin underwater and the blistering kisses. If not for the threat of being discovered by security patrols, she'd have stripped Mickey naked under cover of water and dark of night before you could say "skinny-dipping." The popular recreational activity was Muskoka's best-kept secret.

Precisely at eight o'clock, Rachel tapped discreetly on the Bridal Suite door and, hearing only Mopette's lonely yip-yip, used her master key card. Cautiously she poked her head inside. Fortunately the door to the bedroom remained tightly closed. *If I don't see Candy until we walk down the aisle, that'll be just fine.*

In the Bridal Suite's salon, Mopette joyfully danced on hind legs and pawed the air in welcome, then scurried to retrieve the leash beside her doggy bed.

Rachel hastily surveyed the room for a package of returned laundry containing her underwear, tennis skirt, and halter top. No such luck.

She snapped the leash onto Mopette's jeweled leather collar, scooped the furry pet to her chest, peeked around the door to scan the corridor for chambermaids coming on duty, and then bolted for the exit staircase.

"Mopette," Rachel confided breathlessly as they descended the stairs. "You are *so* lucky dogs get fixed. You'll never be driven half wild with desire for a male who's out of bounds. Forbidden."

Rachel's panting tickled Mopette's ear. The dog shook her head violently.

"Celibacy doesn't appeal to you?" Rachel laughed. "Not to me either. It's a bitch." Mopette whined. "Sorry, girl, I didn't mean you."

Safely through an exit-only fire door at the base of the stairwell and outside at last, Rachel inhaled Muskoka's wonderful fresh, pine-scented air. Photo-taking top of mind, she assessed the weather. The tall pines, maples, and oaks on the property filtered early morning sun. Golden rays streaked the immaculate lawn that sloped to the beach. Beyond, calm ultramarine water stretched for miles. Wispy white clouds floated high above the idyllic setting.

"Mopette, let's pray the forecasted thunderstorms hold off until after the wedding this afternoon."

Anxiety about her role in the day's events had her squeezing the little dog's ribs. Mopette whined in protest. She lowered the dog to the grass. "What's that, Mopette? The bride gets all the attention? Nobody will notice me?"

Mickey noticed you, the pesky inner voice crowed.

Yeah, Mickey might be a problem. He notices everything.

Rachel led Mopette across the lawn beyond visual range of the Bridal Suite windows and guests enjoying morning coffee on the terrace. Behind a massive oak tree Rachel halted to allow the dog to do her business. Mopette obediently squatted.

"*Darn* it, Mopette. I forgot the poop bag again." She pulled the smartphone from her pocket and texted a groundskeeper. "Dog doo alert," she typed. "Northwest front lawn, big old oak tree." It would *not* do for a guest to notice a doggy deposit, let alone step in it by accident.

"You're a sight for sore eyes so early in the morning." The hoarse voice behind her had her jumping out of her teeny bikini.

"Mickey. What a surprise. Halden." Rachel ignored the incoming reply text from the groundskeeper and greeted the two shirtless hunks wearing shorts and sunglasses, both pale and sweaty. Peering more closely, she frowned. "You're both looking…ah…slightly the worse for wear," she ventured.

"Not so loud," Mickey begged with a pained expression. "The men celebrated Halden's last night of freedom before his impeding nuptials." Mickey jabbed a thumb at the panting colossus who'd extended one arm to brace himself against a tree trunk while pulling on a bottle of water. "His first marriage, believe it or not."

"First and only nuptials," Halden grunted, then clamped a massive paw to his forehead. "Speaking hurts my brain."

"A swim, plenty of water to flush out the alcohol, and you'll be good as new," Mickey encouraged.

Halden groaned. "We've run a circuit around the golf course twice. Sweating out the Scotch isn't doing the trick. Candy's going to kill me."

Mickey waved a hand to dismiss the dire prediction. "She won't leave her room for hours. The painkillers will kick in long before then." He absently scratched at a mosquito bite on his arm.

Rachel glanced at the phone in her palm. "According to Wendy's schedule, you're due at the breakfast buffet in forty-five minutes."

Halden groaned. The rumble rolled through the air like thunder. Mopette whined and rubbed up against her master's ankle.

Mickey was unsympathetic. "You didn't trust your bros to keep the bachelor party cool and on the down-low so you made the arrangements. *You* ordered the Scotch whisky direct from the distillery in Scotland. It sure went down smooth. I'm grateful you all started without me, or I'd be in rougher shape myself." He waggled his brows at Rachel above the top of the shades.

Heat crept up her neck. *She'd* made him late for his rendezvous the night before, but the facial contortions aimed at her signified he didn't mind one iota.

Halden glared at Mickey, not appreciating the reminder of his own responsibility for his current condition. "A private bachelor party with male friends and relatives. No girls. No drugs. No damn paparazzi snapping photos that'll haunt my career for the rest of my life. That's all I wanted."

"That's what you got."

"That and a hangover to end all hangovers." Halden nodded emphatically, then rubbed his forehead, regretting the movement. "A quiet wedding today with family and friends. Simple. Private. Relaxed. No pap photos, no media frenzy. Just me and my gal tying the knot for all eternity." He considered. "Oh yeah. One more thing. No splitting headache and nausea would be icing on the wedding cake."

"But publicity helps your career," Rachel exclaimed, taken aback by Halden's declaration. Stars craved attention—the more the better. Why else would they pursue fame?

[♬ "Damned"]

Mickey clapped his buddy's shoulder. "Halden's a Wisconsin good old boy at heart. Why do you think he insisted on staging the wedding outside the US as far as possible from paparazzi without flying over an ocean? He loathes the Hollywood celebrity circus."

Rachel slid the phone into her pocket. Guilt assailed her conscience. Mickey's words rang true, but she looked to Halden for verification.

Halden slitted Nordic ice-blue eyes, glowered under blond brows, straightened to a menacing six foot six, and folded muscular arms across bulging pecs. "If any paps sneak past the security I hired and ruin our big day, I'm going after them myself."

Mopette yipped applause.

Rachel gulped.

Chapter 11

There's Something About Rachel

[♫ "I Wanna Be Loved By You"]

"I wanna be loved by you..." Marilyn Monroe's breathy voice flowed seductively out of speakers hidden in the landscaping around the infinity pool.

Famous beautiful people Rachel'd only ever seen on television or in films chatted, laughed, ate, drank, and enjoyed themselves like regular folks. At the far end of the pool deck, Rachel reclined in a cushioned teak chaise lounge under a large umbrella, her long legs stretched out, feet bare. Incredulously she pinched herself. *Am I seriously being paid to party with movie stars while other chambermaids clean my rooms?*

For the past hour, she'd used the smartphone camera's zoom feature to observe and photograph famous actors. With the patience of a fisherman, she'd pretended to surf and text, waiting for opportune moments to snap stealth photos.

Wendy had produced a Hollywood movie love song challenge. Each brunch guest had been given a souvenir pen engraved with the names "Catherine & Halden" and the wedding date, and a printed card with a list of love songs. After listening to each song, guests were invited to write down the name of the film in which it had been sung. Each person who accurately matched a film title to every song received a $1,000 Nordstrom gift card. Rachel saw no reason she shouldn't be one of them.

Rachel used the slim sterling silver pen to write in the space next to the song title "I Wanna Be Loved By You." The back of the smartphone in her left hand provided a solid surface to write on.

"*Some Like It Hot*," Mickey said at her side.

Startled, Rachel managed a grin. Her heart swelled at the easy smile aimed exclusively at her. Until she became distracted by the love song challenge, she'd tracked his progress around the pool because if anyone noticed her taking photos, it'd be him.

"Already wrote it down." She showed him her card.

He eased onto the adjacent chaise lounge, elbows on knees facing her, and whistled. "You've nailed them all so far."

Mickey wore nothing but navy swim trunks and a pair of sunglasses. His tanned arms and sleek torso glistened with sunscreen. She'd watched him—okay, spied on him using the zoom—schmoozing with the guests. He'd laughed, he'd gestured, he'd air-kissed cheeks, methodically working his way along the three sides of the infinity pool until he reached her. Popular, handsome, charming and confident, Mickey was her polar opposite.

A server swiftly approached, the same snitty girl who'd purposely ignored her all morning except to remove empty dishes. Mickey ordered two glasses of ice water, and the server headed for the outdoor buffet and bar set up under a green-and-white-striped awning near the dining room entrance.

The wedding guests luxuriated in the relative privacy. Some of the celebrities had arrived that morning with their children and nannies. Rachel refused to exploit the adorable children by taking their photos. Crossing that line felt super-disgusting.

Ryan Gosling and his drop-dead gorgeous partner soaked up the sun on matching teak loungers, their daughters fast asleep in a double covered stroller close by. Michael Bublé, the famous Canadian singer, bounced his giggling young children in the shallow end of the saltwater pool. His stunning wife in a white bikini sat on the edge of the pool, dangled her feet in the water, and laughed at their antics.

Several of Halden's guests had starred in blockbuster superhero movies. Cobie Smulders tossed a beach ball in the pool with her young daughter in water wings and handsome husband. Cobie, a Canadian with superhero cred as the voice of Wonder Woman in the 2014 *The Lego Movie*, had played a S.H.I.E.L.D. agent in *Captain America: The Winter Soldier*.

Captain America himself, the buff actor Christopher Evans, remained engrossed in conversation with Halden, Garth, and Tiffany at one of the larger shaded tables. Rachel yearned to overhear Apollo and Captain America's conversation! Chris Evans had a sense of humor; he sported stars-and-stripes swim trunks. Unfortunately the contrast between bright sunshine and heavy shade wiped out facial definition for a phone photo. She'd patiently kept an eye on the group, anticipating that Chris had to move into the sun eventually.

Candy held court with her parents at her side under an umbrella. Halden's relatives ambled over at intervals to pay their respects, but none lingered for more than a few minutes. Clearly Candy did not connect with them on a social level.

No one had noticed Rachel refill her plate twice at the buffet with fruit salad, fluffy scrambled eggs, and French toast slathered in butter and maple syrup. Tiffany, in comparison, washed down a single boiled egg with at least four glasses of champagne and orange juice. Rachel had captured a photo of Garth attempting to hand-feed Tiffany a blueberry as if she were a bird.

The next song rolled out of the speakers. Ewan McGregor and Renée Zellweger sang "Here's to Love."

"*Down with Love*!" Mickey and Rachel blurted simultaneously, then laughed. Rachel scribbled the movie title on her card.

"Do you know the year of the film?" Mickey asked.

"2003." Rachel fished out an ice cube from the glass of water placed at her side and applied it to an especially itchy mosquito bite on her neck that had been driving her crazy all morning. Mindful of the wedding that afternoon, she resisted the urge to scratch. Candy'd have a fit if she saw red welts covering her bridesmaid's exposed skin. And her skin sure had been exposed the previous night. In the lake. With her legs wrapped around Mickey's waist and her tongue down his throat. Heat pooled *down there*. She eyed the infinity pool, longing to jump in and cool off before Mickey twigged to her lustful thoughts.

"Who was the director?"

With difficulty she focused on answering his question. "Peyton Reed. Jeff Cronenweth, *Down with Love*'s cinematographer, was nominated for an Academy Award for *The Girl with the Dragon Tattoo*."

Mickey's dark brows lifted above the rim of his shades. "Impressive. How did you absorb so much arcane movie trivia?"

"I'm a cinephile," she admitted. "There's so much to learn from watching films, even the ones that bomb at the box office."

Mickey swung his legs up onto the adjacent chaise lounge, leaned back, and folded his hands behind his head. "Who has time to watch every movie that opens? Not me, and I'm in the business."

She shrugged. "Eat, sleep, work, watch movies and TV series on my laptop—it's pretty much all I do up here in Muskoka."

"No boyfriend?"

"Boyfriends tie you down."

"Kinky." Speculation had Mickey raising his sunglasses to peer over at her. "Count me in."

Heat flamed—a combo of embarrassment and, frankly, the visual of Mickey tying her wrists to the rustic bent-willow headboard in his room. "You're teasing me. I didn't mean it that way! Honestly." When he shook his head, dismissing her explanation, she added, "I have plans to work in LA after I finish film school."

"Fantastic!" Mickey said, and from his pleased grin he meant it. "I'll show you around, introduce you to a few people."

"You mean as my agent?"

His smile dimmed fractionally. "Sure, if that's what you want. I had a more...*personal* relationship in mind." He waggled the dark brows above his shades suggestively. A delicious flutter rippled down to lodge in her core. He wanted her. Maybe almost as much as she wanted him.

He patted the space on the lounger beside his knees and extended a tanned arm in invitation to join him. Oh, the temptation. A cautious scan of the vicinity, and the prospect of cuddling with Mickey died a quick death. Under the awning by the buffet she discerned the familiar dark-suited shape of the GM on hand to personally monitor the service. She stayed put on her chaise lounge.

"Mickey," she began. "It's a wonderful offer. But I must admit that I haven't yet raised the tuition for the Toronto school's accelerated eighteen-month Film Production program. Although I've been accepted, I may not be able to attend."

Selling the wedding photos was the key to a wonderful future. However, the only daughter of a practical working-class mother never counted her chickens before they hatched.

"Your parents will help, surely?" His nonchalant question presumed every family had thirty grand to throw at their kid's education.

She owed him an explanation that revealed at least part of the difficult truth. "There's just my mom. She…Mom hasn't got a spare nickel." Rachel leaned across the narrow space separating them and squeezed his hand. "As desperately as I wish to move to LA, there's only a slim possibility it'll happen within two years."

He'll never wait for me. The certainty blurred her vision. Her throat constricted. There were thousands of beautiful girls in California. During her eighteen months at film school in Toronto, Mickey'd most likely fall for one, maybe even marry.

Mickey refused to release her hand. "You're young with big dreams. I get that. Have you considered that many roads lead to Rome, or in this case Los Angeles? Off the top of my head, I can name at least three well-respected film schools on the West Coast."

From her research, she'd discovered that annual tuition for foreign students at California state colleges cost *at least* $25,000 more than tuition for American citizens.

When she didn't, couldn't answer, he must've noticed the tears filling her eyes because he added gently, "Let's enjoy this weekend. I'm an optimist. In my business, you only fail when you give up the dream."

The intro to the next song on the list, "I See the Light," tinkled from the speakers. "*Tangled*," she proclaimed with a tremulous smile. "Disney's fiftieth animated movie, song sung by Mandy Moore and Zachary Levi."

"I've never met a girl like you," Mickey said softly. Then he smiled. "You intrigue me." His thumb caressed moisturizer-softened skin on the back of her hand.

The sensual strokes sent silky flutters through sensitized nerves. She drew a shaky breath, glanced everywhere but at him. If Mickey had the ability to kick-start her libido by merely sliding a thumb across a couple of square inches of skin, she dared not imagine what sliding he'd do with her entire body at his disposal. Sliding tongue. Sliding… Background chatter and splashing faded. No one in the world existed except her and Mickey. She leaned to close the space separating their mouths, lips puckered.

"Ahem." An imperious throat-clearing curbed her advance.

Straightening, she squinted at the dark-suited figure a dozen feet away. *Uh-oh. The GM.*

She quickly extracted her hand from Mickey's. Having attracted her attention, the GM discreetly motioned with his head to indicate that she follow him.

She cringed. *This can't be good.* Had he observed her *tête-à-tête* with Mickey? With no shortage of things to be guilty about, her heartbeat ramped up to freeway speed and her worried thoughts shifted into overdrive.

Mr. Chauhan can't fire me before the wedding.

He can put you on notice, her irritating conscience piped up.

Announcing to Mickey that she needed to visit the restroom, Rachel excused herself, slid sore feet into her flip-flops and arms into the transparent cover-up, collected her things, and crossed the sun-heated flagstone pool deck to the dining room door the GM held open for her.

Inside, cool conditioned air hit her like an arctic front, pebbling her skin with goose bumps. She folded her arms across her chest to conceal chilled nipples budding through thin fabric but then thought better of it. She lowered her arms to protectively palm the phone in one pocket and the card and silver pen in the other. Guilt had her biting down hard on her bottom lip.

The GM led her on a winding path between round tables to the farthest corner from the windows and observation, then halted by the swing door to the kitchen. He wore his usual attire—a black suit and pressed white shirt—despite the outdoor eighty-degree Fahrenheit heat. Only the color of the tie changed from day to day. This morning a gold silk tie richly complemented his latte-colored skin.

Rachel's sun-strained eyes failed to interpret his expression in the dim light. Was he furious that she flirted with a guest? Had he spotted her taking photos? Her stomach clenched.

"How is it going, Rachel?" The India-born man spoke precisely, with a slight accent.

"Sir?" The word croaked out of a throat as dry and scratchy as a sand trap on the golf course. Her smartphone contained photos in contravention of his privacy policy, a $1,000 gift card hung in the balance, an irresistibly hot guest tempted her to violate the no hook-up policy, and he wanted to know how *her day* was going? She swallowed with difficulty. "Good," she managed to reply. "I mean, *well.* It's going well."

Muffled music from the outdoor speakers reached them. Ethel Merman belted out *There's No Business Like Show Business.* Was Wendy thinking about Ethel's cover in the 1954 film with the same name, or the original recording? Distracted, Rachel fingered the card in her pocket and anxiously fretted that Wendy's preferred answer might be the 1950 MGM movie *Annie Get Your Gun*, when the song was sung by an ensemble. *Nah, it has to be Ethel's 1954 film.*

"Rachel, I cannot hear you over the rousing music."

Like a doomed sailor walking the plank, she shuffled another foot closer and nervously regarded her boss from under lowered lashes. "Sorry, sir. What may I do for you?"

The GM cleared his throat. "I regret having to interrupt your delightful adventure of being a bridesmaid in a celebrity wedding." The cynical twist to his smile indicated he didn't appear sorry. "However, in case you have not recently spoken to Angeline, I am taking the opportunity to remind you that you must resume your duties early tomorrow morning. Every guest in the hotel is checking out. The room attendants will be hard pressed to turn over every room and suite in time for the three o'clock check-ins Sunday afternoon."

Rachel's chin shot up. "I still have a job?" she squeaked.

His gaze sharpened. He blinked twice. "Why shouldn't you? Is there something I should know?"

At his glacial tone, the hair rose on the back of her neck. The GM had a reputation for OCD attention to detail. Under his management, guest service received top priority, and nothing—no employee, supplier or even the weather—dared compromise that service. His critical eyes raked her from head to toe.

Rachel followed the GM's sight line south to the triangles of fabric scarcely concealing her nipples. Her cheeks burned. "Angeline said you have an unofficial policy about, ah, not hiring pretty room attendants."

The GM's dark eyes widened in shock. Round cheeks bloomed red as tomatoes.

She hastened to calm him and save her job. "The spa makeover is temporary, sir, I assure you. Tomorrow I'll be my regular self. Except for the hair, of course." She automatically raised the hand concealing the card in order to touch the long blond strands but then thought better of it. "The hair color will take months to grow out."

The GM shifted his weight, clearly uncomfortable. His embarrassed regard drifted up and over her head to finally settle on a crystal chandelier. Drawing his shoulders back and posture erect to a pompous five foot six, he cleared his throat. "There is no such policy. That would constitute discrimination. Angeline misunderstood my approach to risk management. Employees are not allowed to engage in, ah, relationships with guests on the premises. *That* is the policy."

It hadn't occurred to Rachel that a manager opened himself up to being accused of discrimination by refusing to hire pretty chambermaids. He might make it an unofficial practice but sure didn't want to be accused of it. One threat to her summer job withered and died. Tense shoulder muscles relaxed fractionally. She released the breath she'd been holding.

After sidestepping that trap, Mr. Chauhan continued. "Rachel, I assure you that with a full hotel in high season, I need every person on staff, including you. Remember your position, behave yourself, and you have nothing to worry about."

"Yes, *sir.*" Behave herself. *Ha.* There lay the rub. As in how Mickey had rubbed her hand on the pool deck. In public. And her skin in the lake. Their affair mustn't go further, per Mr. Chauhan's warning, or he'd give her something to worry about, all right.

He walked stiffly in the direction of the terrace, paused, and swiveled on one polished leather heel to impart final thoughts. "Rachel, if you are transformed into a beauty, I have only myself to blame. I authorized your complimentary spa treatments." A hint of a smile lifted the corner of his mouth and then was quickly suppressed. "I'm counting on your contribution to a successful event," he warned. "Celebrities are good business for this hotel. Their generous gratuities are no doubt very popular with the employees. That will be all."

"Yes, sir. Thank you, sir."

Rachel remained pinned to the floor until he disappeared through the doors to the pool terrace. Then she stumbled on wobbly legs out of the dining room and down the hall to the nearest restroom.

As she washed her hands and splashed her face with cool water, the full impact of the GM's stinging reminder hit her: if Halden and Candy were made unhappy for any reason, the hotel's celebrity business and tips would certainly suffer.

Angeline's four growing kids needed new clothes for school. Her jogging buddy Derek relied on his tips to cover expensive college textbooks. Tears of shame pricked the corners of her eyes.

If I'm doing the right thing for my career by taking the photos, why do I feel like such a horrible, selfish person?

Chapter 12

Can Buy Her Love

Candy adjusted the trailing fabric of the figure-hugging off-white lace wedding gown, dropped a bare shoulder, and pursed her lips into a seductive moue aimed at Raynald's lens—sex and sin in her expression if not in her heart.

Clicking his digital SLR camera shutter rapidly, the tuxedo-attired fashion photographer pranced around her in patent leather shoes—a tall Fred Astaire. "Beautiful," Raynald asserted. "Gorgeous." He snapped shots from several angles.

"The photos better be," Candy said without moving her mouth or muscles in her face, skills she'd acquired during years of fashion shoots in Milan, Paris, and New York City. She twisted to look over her shoulder, lashes lowered. The lace of her gown shimmered with a thousand tiny crystals hand sewn to the fabric.

They were alone. She'd ordered Wanda to remove Mopette from the Bridal Suite while Raynald snapped sexy photos half an hour before the three o'clock wedding. Much as she loved Mopette, Candy didn't want her dog's sharp little claws anywhere near the gown for fear of tearing the outrageously expensive Irish lace.

“Darling, trust me. Have I ever let you down? You’ll get what you need,” Raynald purred.

“The bank manager had the nerve to text me yesterday about the two missed loan payments. The day before my wedding!”

“Wicked.” Raynald’s voice vibrated with outrage.

“I know, right?” Candy angled her cleavage at the vanity mirror, pretended to adjust the white baby’s breath woven through intricately coiled hair. A gossamer veil and tiara glittering with Austrian Swarovski crystals—a gift from her mother—dangled from her ring finger, the real diamond strategically aimed to catch the light.

[♬ “Can’t Buy Me Love”]

“Why don’t you simply ask Halden for fifty grand to cover the overdue loan payments?” Raynald clicked the shutter rapidly.

Candy consciously released tension that creased her—so far—Botox-free brow at his impertinent question. “And confirm his family’s suspicion I’m marrying Halden for his fame and money?” She placed freshly manicured toes on the vanity footstool, arched her back, and pleated the floor-length fabric along her thigh to reveal a blue satin lace-trimmed garter.

“Aren’t you?”

“Raynald! Not you too?” After years of working together, the fashion insider understood her too well. She wanted Raynald’s help, not judgment. Candy silkened her tone. “I adore Halden. He’s so sweet. There isn’t a cynical bone in that fabulous body.”

“His body *is* fabulous,” Raynald agreed with an envious sigh. “Smile for me, darling. You’re in love.”

"Damn right I'm in love!"

And she *did* love Halden, even more than she cherished Mopette. His genuine emotions and open heart balanced her east coast cynicism and pragmatic nature. When she'd maneuvered to meet Halden at a party four months earlier, she'd fallen for him, and *not* because the *Apollo* film franchise had made him fabulously wealthy.

Fashion industry gossip labeled her a washed-up gold digger. She intended to prove them wrong by reinventing herself into a successful entrepreneur at the head of Candy Kane Cosmetics. If her company went under, she'd not only be mired in major debt but also ridiculed as a failure.

"Halden mustn't find out that if the bank calls the loan next week, my business will go into receivership." She abandoned her pose. Fear manifested in crinkling of carefully applied lipstick. "He believes in me. He thinks I'm perfect. He even refused Garth and his lawyer's advice to make me sign a prenup."

"If he only knew." Raynald swung his head at Halden's naiveté.

"Knew what?" She fussed with the draping of the fragile lace fabric, her attention on assuming a new pose on the upholstered stool at the vanity.

"How sharp you are," Raynald improvised. "How brilliant. You're a beautiful woman with a brain for business, running a thriving private company."

"That's precisely what he believes, and I want to keep it that way."

After several deep, calming yoga breaths to quell uneasiness twisting her stomach, Candy scrutinized her flawlessly made-up face in the vanity mirror for any trace of tension. She assumed a seductive smile. After so many years as a runway and commercial photography model, masking emotions became second nature. *In less than an hour I'll be Mrs. Halden Armstrong.*

"Men are so insecure. Ask him before the wedding to bail me out? Plant the seed that his money is my motivation for being with him, that I'm yet another celebrity leech? Impossible. I have no choice, really."

"Darling, your sister Gwendolyn is dating that fabulously rich North Sea oil magnate. To him, fifty grand is petty cash."

"Gwendy is dead to me," Candy spat. "She stole Sir Timothy Snifton from me at a gala in his honor in London. Do not *ever* speak her name in my presence. Or the name Wendy, for that matter. The mention of it puts me in a pissy mood."

Raynald tutted-tutted. "You're looking at this the wrong way, darling. You won. The minimal media attention Sir Snifton gets is in the stock market news and when he donates to disaster relief or a charity. He's practically invisible. Show me that smile of triumph."

Candy obliged. The tension in her shoulders and neck eased. "You're absolutely correct."

Raynald crouched at her knees and snapped several close-ups. "Halden is rich *and* famous. You're the envy of half the women in America." He hesitated. "Won't you receive scads of expensive wedding gifts? Surely you can return them for cash."

Candy's professional smile wavered. "Halden said *I* am the most wonderful gift he could possibly receive. He insisted that the wedding invitations specify that, in lieu of gifts, donations be made to his Save the Whales campaign. He hopes to set a precedent."

Raynald clucked sympathetically. "He's a generous man. It's getting *at* the cash that's the difficulty, hummm?"

Candy wasn't finished. "Halden has a weird obsession with the enormous sea creatures," she hissed through lips stretched over gritted teeth. "I had to agree or appear petty. Is it so awful for a bride to receive a few gifts? The *whales* won't receive a penny. It all goes into the pockets of international government *lobbyists*." The last sentence came out on a wavering breath perilously close to a sob.

Raynald straightened and lowered his camera. "Darling, you're appallingly tense. We're finished for the moment. You *must* relax." He reached to pat the hand trembling under the weight of the flashy $50,000 diamond. "Leave everything to me."

★★★★★

Sweat trickled down Mickey's temples. The groom and his groomsmen stood in formation to the right of the white-painted gazebo, with Halden nearest the step, and Mickey at the other end. Under the cone-shaped roof decorated with garlands of purple and white flowers, the bald pastor from the Armstrong family's hometown church cooked in his black robe and white collar. He held the family bible in two plump hands and shifted his considerable weight from foot to foot.

The invitingly cool blue lake stretched for miles in the distance. No breeze stirred the surface nor offered relief to the hundred or so perspiring guests awaiting the bride.

Halden and the groomsmen wore dark formal tailcoats, striped gray trousers, white shirts, and lavender cravats and waistcoats. At intervals during the interminable delay, they bemoaned the wedding planner's order for traditional English attire. Who knew it'd be as hot as hell in June in the Great White North? Apparently not the wedding planner or Candy. Or more likely they didn't care. To them, it was all about appearances.

"She's twenty frigging minutes late." Garth inserted one finger inside his collar and tugged at the garment constricting his neck. "If I ever get married, it'll be in January."

"Make it February fourteenth," Mickey muttered out the side of his mouth. "Then you'll never forget your wedding anniversary."

"Good tip. You always think ahead, Mick." Garth fist-bumped him behind Wade's back.

A thick white carpet covered the uneven flagstone path from the gazebo to the hotel, dividing rows of white wooden chairs. The women wore colorful summer dresses and fancy hats that had somehow escaped crushing in baggage, the men summer-weight suits, shirts, and ties. The nannies had squirreled away the children for naps or spirited them off to the playground beside the tennis courts, out of sight and hearing.

Garth patted the beads of sweat on his forehead with a pressed cotton handkerchief. "Hey, Mickey and Wade. In your room last night after the bachelor party, did either of you find rose petals scattered on your bed and a bottle of red wine with a note on hotel stationery?"

Mickey suppressed a chuckle. "No," he managed. "How 'bout you, Wade?" He stepped out of line to aim a broad wink at Wade, which he carefully concealed from Garth. Halden ignored them, his eyes trained on the hotel's rear entrance.

Wade accepted Mickey's invitation to play along. "Not me. Apparently I don't rate the special night service. What did the note say?"

"It was handwritten. 'Compliments of Juanita from Reception. If you want anything, please call,' with the word 'anything' underlined twice and a phone number."

Wade whistled.

Mickey yanked at his cravat to give his damp neck some air. "That Juanita is incredibly beautiful, not to mention stacked. Seems clear she has the hots for you. Well, did you call her?"

Garth shot back, "Are you nuts? Tiffany's the gal for me." He cast a suspicious scowl at his friends. "I'd sure like to get my hands on the joker who planted the idea in that woman's head that I'd be interested in a hook-up." A circuit connected in his big brain. "Hey, Mick, how'd *you* know anything about Juanita's looks?"

[♫ "Bridal Chorus"]

The traditional "Here Comes the Bride" wedding march blared from speakers concealed in the gazebo ceiling, saving Mickey from further interrogation. *En masse* the guests swiveled in their seats for a view of the procession from the hotel.

Mickey shaded his eyes under a hand. Candy, via her wedding planner mouthpiece, had banned sunglasses for the wedding party. Rachel, a willowy vision in pale lavender chiffon and holding a large bouquet at her waist, emerged from the hotel, followed by Tiffany and Asta. The two bridesmaids synced their pace to Rachel's slow, cautious lead across the terrace on the white carpet.

Mickey willed Rachel not to stumble in her heels on the uneven surface. Concern that Tiff's careful steps indicated she'd been drinking had him squinting into bright sunlight on high alert. He'd attended several parties at which Tiffany had had difficulty standing, let alone walking in those high heels women insisted on wearing.

As Rachel planted one foot in front of the other at a stately pace down the carpeted aisle between the seated guests, he forgot all about Tiffany, never even noticing the moment the bride appeared. A coronet of white roses graced shining blond hair that fell loose to Rachel's bare shoulders. Petite, perfect breasts swelled above the strapless bodice. Her rosebud lips parted in a smile in his direction, although logic dictated she couldn't distinguish one groomsman from another due to pathetic distance vision.

Mickey's heart pounded like a drum under the shirt and vest. His groin swelled, stiffened. He'd believed women dragged men to the altar. Never again. The will to forge a permanent link with such loveliness overrode common sense, overrode thoughts of possible consequences. In the moment, nothing else mattered except a guarantee this woman would be at his side every day, in his bed every night.

And unavailable to other men.

He glanced at Halden, fiercely intent on his approaching bride, and understood at last why Halden had agreed to a short engagement. Candy, a vision of radiant light and elegance reminiscent of Lady Galadriel in the *Lord of the Rings* film franchise, floated ethereally down the aisle on the arm of her tall, thin father. A glittering tiara rested on blond hair braided and coiled in Scandinavian fashion, a nod to Halden's heritage. Her figure-hugging lace gown sparkled and shimmered with every step. No veil covered her face. To provide photographers with better shots, he concluded uncharitably.

As Candy drew near, he realized Halden and Wade hadn't even noticed Rachel or the other bridesmaids. Nor had the guests. The princess bride drew all eyes. Cameras clicked. Candy's friend Raynald elbowed aside the official photographer and folded spindly limbs in a grasshopper crouch on the carpet for frontal shots.

Mickey struggled with a crazy impulse to grab Rachel's hand and tug her into the gazebo to stand with him before the pastor. An unthinking step in her direction to do exactly that flash-froze the hormones coursing through his veins. Realization that the ceremony was underway slammed him back into line with the other men.

Holy Fork in the Road. He'd fallen hook, line, and sinker for Candy's Canadian cousin.

The easy attraction and potential for a weekend affair instantaneously morphed into something astonishingly serious. Because not only did he want Rachel in his bed, he wanted her at his side, hand in hand, facing that pastor.

His life had suddenly become impossibly complicated.

Chapter 13

His Best Friend's Wedding

Rachel stepped carefully off the carpet and onto the grass to the left of the two steps up to the gazebo platform. The three inch heels of the ill-fitting pumps dyed to match the dress didn't sink into parched turf and throw her off balance, thank the gods. However, the shoes exerted tortuous pressure on her blistered, swollen toes.

The photos were worth the agony. *Twenty thousand dollars.* The amount ran though her mind like lyrics to the "Bridal Chorus" spilling from hidden speakers.

When she reached the precise location assigned in the previous day's rehearsal, she raised her chin and squinted across at the groomsmen. Spellbound, she blatantly stared. Mickey appeared as suavely debonair as Hugh Grant in *Four Weddings and a Funeral,* and even more distinguished thanks to Mickey's silver-threaded dark hair. His boutonnière consisted of an ivory rose nestled in spears of lavender, harmonizing with the white roses, lavender spears, and delicate baby's breath in the bridesmaids' bouquets.

Bouquet! Her breath hitched.

The walk down the aisle had demanded utmost concentration, driving out all thoughts of the smartphone secretly stashed in her bouquet. She discreetly dropped her gaze to inspect the bouquet. To her immense relief, a glint of the silver phone case confirmed that it remained camouflaged deep within the exquisite arrangement, camera app open. She ignored the self-reproach twisting her stomach.

Twenty thousand dollars. La, la, la, la. Twenty thou-sand dollars.

Mickey, in line on the opposite side of the carpet, caught her eye and grinned. At this crucial juncture, she'd much rather he watch the ceremony, not her. Lavender supposedly relieved stress. Rachel inhaled the delicate fragrance wafting from the flowers in the bouquets and hung in garlands from the roof of the circular gazebo. A shaking forefinger delved between rose stems and into position by the shutter button.

Beside her, Tiffany and Asta assumed their positions to form one half of a V, like Canada geese flying in formation. Candy grandly sashayed between the bridesmaids on one side and the groomsmen on the other. Mr. Kane air-kissed his daughter's cheek and handed her off to Halden.

The bride and groom ascended the two steps into the gazebo, followed by Asta and Wade, Tiffany and Garth, and then finally herself and Mickey. On the circular platform, the bridesmaids and groomsmen parted to reassemble on the bride's and groom's sides, respectively. Candy transferred to Asta the satin-wrapped stems of her elaborate cascading bouquet of ivory roses, fluffy white peonies, iris, soft lavender, and trailing vines.

Showtime.

The minister switched on his microphone, and the members of the wedding party shuffled into forward-angled positions as rehearsed. Rachel rapidly assessed the angles and adjusted the position of her bouquet. To her amazement, the stars aligned, literally, presenting to her hidden camera an unobstructed view of Halden's love-sick expression as he regarded the beautiful woman at his side.

[♫ "Wedding Day"]

As practiced in the bathroom while waiting for Candy earlier, Rachel aimed the camera lens through a prearranged gap in the roses. She pressed the silent shutter button, capturing Halden's full-face radiant grin of pure joy and Candy's adoring smile in profile.

Halden's eyes misted and then glossed swimming pool blue. Press.

A tear rolled like a boulder down one cheek. Press. *Woo-hoo!* An intimate, emotional portrait of Apollo crying! The money shot!

Halden enfolded his bride's hand in his, and in unison they turned to face the pastor, their backs to the audience. And her camera.

The music ended. The minister's gentle words about love and commitment, amplified by the mic, filled the air. Self-reproach shoved its way through Rachel's feelings of triumph.

You're seriously going to profit from Halden's emotional vulnerability? Judas.

Rachel's elated smile wavered. *Shut up! He's an actor. He's paid to display emotions to the world.*

Her relentless conscience refused to be squelched. *Halden is* not *acting. He came all the way to Muskoka to ensure a private wedding. What kind of person reveals a man's intimate moments to the world for money?*

Rachel stiffened. *I don't want to hurt anyone. That's not who I am. He'll never find out it was me.*

Are you absolutely certain of that? her conscience rejoined. *Even if Halden never finds out, I will haunt you forever because you paid for film school by exploiting Halden's wedding photos.*

Rachel's shoulders sagged under the twenty thousand pounds of guilt she'd assume if she sold the photos. "I can't do it." The whisper leaked out under cover of the minister's droning recital of a poem extolling the marital bond. Before she could change her mind, the forefinger inside the bouquet powered off the phone.

In less time than it took to say "I do," her career track switched from that of a Hollywood cinematographer to a job in a big-box store photography studio. *Passport photos anyone?*

Her entire body trembled with the effort to hold back tears. Still, the weight of the mistake she'd dodged slid off her shoulders as easily as the hundred pound waterlogged robe Mickey'd removed when he saved her from drowning the previous evening.

Darling Mickey.

On the opposite side of the gazebo, Mickey cocked his head and raised his eyebrows in an "anything wrong" query. Her movements must've distracted him from the ceremony because he'd no way of sensing her inner turmoil. Or that her decision seconds ago meant she'd never move out to LA to work, would never see him after this weekend.

Rachel rapidly blinked away sorrowful tears for what might have been. To appease him, she assumed the sweet but sexy smile she'd practiced. *Suck it up, Lehmann. Look happy*, she instructed herself. *It's a joyous occasion.*

Reassured, Mickey directed his attention to the minister's speech.

Rachel sniffed softly and straightened her bouquet. The proof that true love existed outside of movies was *something* to hold on to at least. That and the $1,000 Nordstrom gift card that Wendy had handed her at noon for accurately completing the Hollywood love song challenge. Better to count her blessings than bemoan might-have-beens.

When the minister asked for the rings, Candy's spindly fashion photographer friend, Raynald, nudged Rachel's backside as he squeezed between the edge of the platform and the bridesmaids for a good camera angle. Halden's thunderous Apollo glare from under spliced brows drove the photographer off the platform to a safe distance on the lawn. Rachel hadn't noticed Raynald while fixated on capturing photos of Halden and Candy. Although his presence in the gazebo annoyed Halden, she could hardly fault Raynald for sharing the same objective.

The minister intoned into the microphone clipped to his robe, "The groom will speak his vows."

Halden had announced at the rehearsal the previous afternoon that he'd personalized the traditional phrases and had insisted on saving them for the ceremony. He'd firmly refused the wedding planner's entreaties to wear a microphone. His vows were to be private. Now the time had arrived.

Halden gently supported Candy's long, delicate fingers in his right plate-sized palm and regarded her with loving intensity. At his nod, the minister switched off his microphone.

Halden's low emotion-roughened timbre only reached the ears of those in the gazebo. "My heart belongs to you, my darling. I fell in love with you the night we met. Although we're both accustomed to the glare of camera lighting, I promise to guard our family's privacy, to be honest and authentic with you always, to be a good father to our children, and to be a faithful, loving friend and husband, in sickness and in health, as long as we both shall live."

Garth passed Halden a platinum band studded with tiny diamonds, which he slid onto Candy's finger. "With this ring, I wed you."

Sentimental tears pooled under Rachel's mascara-heavy lashes. An enormous lump prevented her from swallowing. She lifted the end of a lavender satin ribbon dangling from the wrapped stem of her bouquet to dab the corners of her eyes. Garth, the emotional big lug, gruffly cleared his throat. Mickey caught her eye, aiming her way a solemn twist to his lips instead of his characteristic charming smile.

Candy raised her left hand to admire the sparkling band bracketing her engagement ring, her triumphant smile a counterpoint to her lover's enraptured grin. The crystals in her tiara dramatically flashed in the sun. From the perspective of those behind the couple, she appeared to be a twinkling fairy tale princess hovering in golden light against a backdrop of crystal blue sky and water. The celebrity wedding planner was good, but not good enough to arrange *that* spectacular effect.

Asta slid a gold ring practically the diameter of the Canadian dollar coin off a thumb and into Candy's palm. The minister's reactivated microphone amplified Candy's clear soprano for all to hear.

"My darling, I love your talent, your energy, your strength, and how incredibly handsome you are." In the audience a few women sighed. "But I *fell* in love with your pure and beautiful soul. You make me a better person. With you I feel whole. Together we can accomplish anything. I pledge to be faithful to you and to love you with all my heart, in sickness and in health, so long as we both shall live."

A rustle in the audience signaled hankies being pulled from clutch purses and jacket pockets. An excited "yip-yip" from the last row of chairs drew attention to Mopette clutched in Wendy's arms. Laughing musically, Candy swiveled to locate her dog. With the hand holding the ring, she blew a kiss to Mopette. Chuckles rippled through the audience.

Aglow with happiness, the bride slid the wide band onto Halden's third finger. "With this ring, I thee wed."

Halden lowered his head to kiss her. Before their lips touched, Candy laid a staying hand on his arm. Impatient, Halden cued the minister with a sharp glance.

"I now pronounce you husband and wife. You may kiss the bride." The minister nodded to Halden.

Halden gathered Candy to him and lifted her off her feet in a passionate, enthusiastic embrace. The crowd applauded. After thoroughly smudging Candy's lipstick, Halden gently released her. Hand in hand, as rehearsed, they faced the gathered guests.

"I present to you Mr. and Mrs. Halden Armstrong." The minister's words trumpeted from the speakers.

[♫ "Wedding March"]

Jubilant music flooded the air. In unison the audience rose to applaud in a standing ovation spiced with whoops and whistles from the groomsmen and Halden's male family members.

Halden's hands encircled his bride's tiny waist, and he effortlessly swung her from the gazebo to the carpet. With her hand tucked into his elbow, Halden escorted Candy to the flagstone terrace for the receiving line. Behind the couple, the paired bridesmaids and groomsmen, followed by the minister, made up the rest of the recession.

In the receiving line, Halden, Candy, their parents, and the attendants acknowledged the guests' congratulations and effusive compliments for the beautiful bride, and exchanged air kisses. Cameras clicked like crickets. Guests who'd paid their respects scattered to check on their children or wandered over to tables where a traditional English afternoon tea—tiered caddies of finger sandwiches, scones, and tiny cakes—offered refreshment. Servers circulated with containers of hot or iced tea.

Stationed at the tail end of the receiving line, Rachel pinched herself to verify it wasn't all a dream. Actors she'd adored in films or on television politely offered their hands to shake. Beyond excited, she breathlessly exchanged greetings with star after star and their companions.

When the last couple in line, Halden's aunt and uncle from Wisconsin, introduced themselves, Rachel smiled and politely explained that she was Candy's cousin from Toronto. She'd repeated the lie so often, she almost believed it herself.

The attractive, naturally blond, blue-eyed woman imprisoned Rachel's hand. "Rachel, dear, Candy's family is our family. I'll be very glad to invite you to stay with Dave and me for the next Armstrong family reunion."

"Oh." Rachel's mind blanked. "Thank you so much," she managed, cheeks flaming, feeling like the worst jerk for misleading such nice people.

"We'll keep in touch," Dave added.

Duty done, the very warm male half of the couple loosened his tie with a heartfelt grunt of relief and allowed his wife to propel him toward the fancy food on the terrace "only if I can order a beer."

The wedding planner hastened over to update those in the receiving line on where and when to assemble for the formal photo-shoot. Then she escorted Candy, Halden, Asta, Garth, and the minister indoors to sign the marriage documents.

Mickey gently nudged Rachel's shoulder. In a low voice audible only to her, he said, "I didn't take my eyes off you up there. I want to speak with you alone."

Her spirits tumbled off a cliff. *Oh my gods!* Eagle-eyed Mickey must have noticed her fiddling with the phone camera hidden in the bouquet.

Chapter 14

Gone with the Dog

Mickey grabbed Rachel's free hand and pulled her behind an old oak. His pained expression signaled she was in for it, no mistake. For long seconds he merely searched her flushed face, mute.

She bit her lip, avoided perceptive steel-gray eyes that missed nothing, and held her breath, awaiting the accusation. In her other hand, the flowers in her bouquet shook. She shoved it behind her back, willing the hidden smartphone not to dislodge and fall out at her feet.

Unable to bear the suspense any longer, Rachel quavered, "What is it?"

"You're one of a kind, Rachel." At her worried frown, he clarified, "You're not fake like these Hollywood girls. You're the real deal."

"Nothing fake about these babies." Rachel ducked her chin to her minuscule breasts.

He chuckled. "Did I mention funny?" He enfolded her free hand in both of his and leaned in, his firm, delicious lips a breath from hers. "Beautiful, talented, intelligent, *funny*—you're the entire package."

Rachel quirked a skeptical brow. No one had ever said those words to her. *No one. Ever.*

"I mean it." He cleared his throat and hastily surveyed the area to ensure privacy. "I've been thinking about us."

"Us?" she squeaked with unabashed surprise. She met his eyes at last. No laugh lines crinkled the corners. He appeared serious.

"After this weekend."

"After the weekend?" she repeated like a moron.

"Our future," he explained patiently.

Her jaw dropped. "Together?"

"Well, not immediately," he amended, thinking aloud. "You'll have to be accepted at a film school in LA, apply for a student visa, and move out to California in September." He dropped a quick kiss on lips parted in astonishment. "I believe in you, Rachel. I don't want us to end tomorrow when I jump on that plane. I want to explore a relationship. How about you?"

Dumbfounded, her head whirled. The words *I'm not who you think I am. I'm a broke chambermaid* swirled up her throat. Firmly clamped jaws prevented their escape. Her eyes filmed with sadness that mourned the impossible future Mickey dangled like a happy ending in a Hollywood movie.

"What are you feeling, Rach?" Mickey raised her hand to kiss work-reddened skin that the expensive spa moisturizer could not repair. "Tell me."

What am I feeling? She had no words to express the powerful emotions dueling in her heart. Her decision during the ceremony meant that she could not afford to attend film school in Toronto or anywhere else. Besides, Mickey'd drop her in a microsecond if he ever discovered she was only a maid. Gods willing, she'd fool him for one more day. Longer than that? Unthinkable.

"Yoo-hoo. Mickey. Rachel. I've been searching everywhere." The wedding planner's voice warbled from the carpet a short distance from the oak tree. She waved them over.

Rachel blew out a tremulous breath. *Whew.* Saved from manufacturing another lie by the wedding planner's timely arrival.

"We'll resume this conversation later," Mickey vowed.

The planner had already collected Wade and Asta. When Mickey and Rachel joined the small group, the middle-aged woman pointed to the granite slope at the far end of the beach. "The wedding party is due at the Rockery scenic outlook for the formal wedding photo-shoot. Follow the stone-dust path the length of the beach and wait for the bride and groom."

★★★★★

A few minutes later, Mickey, Rachel, Wade, and Asta joined Tiffany and Garth at the Rockery. The wedding planner had remained behind to round up the bridal couple.

Rachel surveyed the location with dismay. An undulating outcrop of gray-pink granite sloped to the water's edge, capping one end of the sand beach. Located at the other end of the beach were the docks and boathouse with kayaks, canoes, pedal boats, and life jackets for guests' use.

The highest point of the Rockery presented an unobstructed view of the lake. Heat radiated from a flat concrete surface through the thin soles of Rachel's shoes. The observation platform had been soaking up rays all day. Wilting potted flowers and greenery decorated the granite incline down to the water. Staff had removed all the Muskoka chairs from the concrete outlook and arranged them in a semicircle on the lawn under shade umbrellas.

What was the wedding planner thinking when she chose this location? Didn't solid rock heat like an oven under California sun? Aloud Rachel merely observed, "The temperature must be at least thirty degrees Celsius up here."

Garth confirmed her guess. "According to my smartphone, the temperature is ninety degrees Fahrenheit."

An electric golf cart with Halden at the wheel rolled silently along the beachside path and braked at the base of five flagstone steps to the level concrete outlook. The wedding planner hopped off the back and scurried to extract Candy from the passenger seat without damaging the gown's fragile lace.

Showtime.

The official wedding photographer, a middle-aged man in a black polo shirt and tan chinos, requested that the assembled wedding party and guests silence all mobile phones. He deftly adjusted the positions of the bride and groom against a backdrop of powder-blue sky dissolving into azure lake.

Awaiting their turn in front of the camera tripod, Rachel, Asta, and Tiffany perched on stools under a large umbrella, dabbing at sweat-beaded skin with handkerchiefs supplied by the photographer's assistant. Marie-Eve from the hotel spa hovered to touch up makeup and hair.

On the lawn facing the concrete "stage", the bride's and groom's parents and Halden's aunts and uncles patiently awaited their turn in front of the camera. A dozen friends of the couple had wandered over from the inn to observe. Derek, Rachel's server pal, served frosty beer, water, and fruit juices from an ice cream cart repurposed as a drinks cooler. Candy's friend Raynald wandered here and there snapping candid shots of the guests and wedding party.

Satisfied with the bridal couple's positions, the official photographer retreated to crouch behind his camera. Rachel credited him with a very professional strategy. The digital camera on his lowered tripod tilted slightly above horizontal, thus recording only sky behind the subjects. If a jet condensation trail or bird appeared in the background, he'd easily Photoshop it out in postproduction.

Over the next half hour, Rachel watched with professional interest during a long series of shots of the bride and groom alone, with their attendants, and in men-only and women-only groups. The wedding photographer's cute assistant, in a pink polka-dotted sundress and sneakers, scurried at his command to adjust ties, shoulder angles, dress fabric, and bouquets. Marie-Eve swooped in during setups with powder and brushes to dust away shine on heated faces.

For class assignments in her two-year commercial photography program, Rachel had photographed indoor and outdoor weddings. Outdoor photography was technically much more difficult. Despite preparations, a photographer had no control over ambient lighting. Wind created havoc with hair.

Until that afternoon, Rachel had considered her commercial photography training to be merely a stepping stone to a camera operator career. The other graduates sought entry-level positions as studio and wedding photographers or videographers. Without the money for film school—that dream dead despite Mickey's unrealistic plans—shooting weddings was a step up from cleaning hotel rooms, for sure. *Something to think about after this fantasy weekend...*

Fingers crossed that she'd not be called out for messing up a group shot, Rachel risked an eye roll at the sky. Late-afternoon puffy clouds dark with evaporated lake water foreshadowed wet weather later that evening unless the wind picked up and blew rain clouds inland.

Rachel grumpily decided that modeling under hot lights, or in this case blazing sun, had to be one of the most uncomfortable jobs ever. The fussy photographer's endless adjustments prolonged what should have been an hour shoot.

Where the heck did the glamor come in? Her cheek muscles hurt from sustaining the fake smile. Her ankles and toes throbbed from balancing on a hard surface in heels. Prickling heat on her shoulders warned of a nasty sunburn. The wedding planner had refused to allow the bridesmaids to apply sunscreen in case it stained the dresses.

Bored with observing countless poses of the bride and groom with and without attendants, Candy's and Halden's relatives and friends chatted quietly in the shade. Wendy loitered with Mopette on a leash, on standby for photos with Candy. Marie-Eve had returned to the hotel to replenish her supply of cosmetics.

"Ms. York, please straighten your bouquet," coaxed the photographer. His assistant scurried over burning concrete to Tiffany.

Rachel risked a glance at the woman beside her. Tiffany's bouquet lolled sideways. In fact, so did Tiffany's head. *Uh-oh.*

Faster than you could say "brie," Tiffany's legs collapsed under her. She sank bonelessly to the ground, the voluminous skirt forming a lavender chiffon pouf. Her torso slumped forward. Her forehead hit the concrete with a dull *thunk.*

Oh my gods! The gallery's gasp echoed Rachel's horror.

Asta, Halden, and the groomsmen swarmed the fallen angel, shoving Rachel aside. She placed her bouquet carefully on the low sweep of granite beside a flowerpot and hurried to help.

"Call a doctor," Garth thundered. He squatted to gather Tiffany in his arms.

"Don't move her!" Wendy had the presence of mind to yell. She pushed her way through the people crowding the unconscious bridesmaid. "Possible head injury. Stand back. I'm trained in first aid." Her authoritative tone inspired confidence.

Because the extent of Rachel's medical knowledge involved treating bug bites and blisters, she left the field to Wendy. Candy wailed like a wild thing, adding to the pandemonium. Halden corralled his new wife, escorting her away from the scene to the shade of an umbrella on the lawn. A male uniformed security guard burst from the thicket of trees on the run. Abandoning Candy, Halden intercepted him. The two men barked into their phones, waving to catch the attention of the man at the helm of the patrol boat speeding to shore.

Rachel noticed Derek's lanky figure quit the drinks cart and make a beeline for the hotel while speaking into his mobile phone. She left the outlook, kicked off her pumps and flew across the grass in her bare feet after him.

When within reach, she grabbed his shirt. "Derek," she panted, "is that the GM?"

"Yeah. I asked him whether I should call 911. He said he'd do it."

"I'm pretty sure Halden's security team has that covered." She appropriated Derek's phone, identified herself, and flinched at the loud, agitated squawk that emanated from the speaker. "A bridesmaid fainted, yes. Tiffany York. Sir, can you check with Reception to find out if one of the guests is a physician?" Candy's piercing screech made her wince. "Or a psychologist? Ms. Kane's having a meltdown." She shook her head. "Or rather, I mean the new Mrs. Armstrong."

The oppressive heat, Mopette's excited yapping, and the bride's shrieks made it difficult to think. "What's that noise you hear?" She squinted at the source, but at that distance Candy merely appeared to be a whirling, sparkling blur on the lawn. "No idea, sir."

Derek snatched the phone to give the GM a play-by-play. "The bride is hitting that skinny photographer with her bouquet. Flowers are flying everywhere. No, sir. She's flailing the *guest* photographer, not the hired guy. He tried to take pictures of her throwing a fit. Could be he's injured too. Rose thorns and whatnot." He listened for a second, eagerly watching the action. "Yes, sir, the *bride* beat on the guest. But it's stopped. The groom pinned the bride's arms, and the hired security manhandled the photographer a safe distance away."

Derek listened to the agitated voice for a few more seconds, then signed off. He flashed her a huge grin. She guessed the photo-shoot disaster made a welcomed change from the tedium of serving drinks.

Drawing his shoulders back importantly, he relayed, "The GM wants you and me to stay at the scene to coordinate the hotel staff response. He'll be on his way after he alerts Juanita at Reception and gives instructions to the doorman for the paramedics. He's gonna try to fend off the police, but hey, don't they have to show up on 911 calls?" With a brief nod and a "you look totally hot in that frou-frou dress, Rachel," he reversed direction and sprinted back to his station at the Rockery.

Rachel padded slowly across the grass after him. When she arrived at the concrete outlook, Mopette trotted up, leash trailing, lavender satin bow askew between her ears, little pink tongue lolling out of the side of her mouth. She yipped a happy greeting. *At least Candy's dog is having a good time.*

Mickey detached from the group that protectively surrounded Tiffany and jogged over. He stamped a foot on the trailing leash, his features pinched with worry, sweat dripping down his face. He'd ditched the formal jacket and rolled up the sleeves of the damp white shirt plastered to his skin. One end of his cravat dangled from his striped trousers' left pocket.

When Mopette danced on her hind legs to paw at Rachel's dress, Mickey tugged on the leash and saved the chiffon from the tiny claws.

"Halden asked me to secure the dog," he explained. "He had his hands full with Candy."

"No kidding. I heard. We all heard." She raised a palm to shade her eyes from strong western rays and squinted over at the blurry figures encircling the fallen bridesmaid.

Behind the drinks cart, Candy sobbed brokenly in her mother's arms, tiara askew. Flowers from Candy's demolished bouquet littered the lawn. Rachel cynically figured Candy to be more freaked about the ruined wedding photos than Tiffany's health but dared not repeat it aloud.

Instead she reported, "Derek called the hotel. The paramedics are on their way. They'll be here in ten minutes."

"How do *you* know that?" Mickey wound Mopette's leash around his hand. "And who's Derek?"

"The server." She gestured in the direction of the drinks cart. "He, ah, says the hotel's only ten minutes from Port Carson, the nearest town."

He acknowledged the info with a curt nod of his firm jaw. "I'll inform Garth and Halden. Then help me push the gawkers back to give Tiff space. She's still out cold. Garth's frantic."

Together they urged the concerned guests to return to their seats, and then positioned themselves in the shade at a distance to keep Mopette out of the way yet close enough to observe the action. The photographer and his assistant packed up their gear.

Garth, Wade, and Asta protectively encircled the unconscious bridesmaid. Wendy knelt at her side and pressed a handkerchief soaked in cold water to her deathly pale forehead and cheeks. Garth had stripped off his jacket and carefully slid it between the concrete and her head. Wendy called for a shade umbrella. Derek hurried to comply.

Barely audible above the worried chatter, Tiffany moaned. Black lash extensions fluttered like spider legs on chalk-white skin. "What happened?" she slurred. "I want to sit up."

"Wait a minute or two, Tiffany," Wendy suggested.

"Now!"

Wendy gently supported Tiffany's back as she rose to a sitting position. Tiffany promptly bent and vomited all over Garth's jacket.

"Thank the Lord, she's conscious," Garth bellowed to his parents. Halden interrupted his consultations with the security team and ran over to see for himself.

A disheveled Raynald shoved his camera between Wade's and Garth's broad shoulders. Garth drew back a sledgehammer fist. "You've had this coming all day, you rude devil."

"Garth, you're not helping," Wendy barked. "Please get Tiffany a glass of water."

Reluctantly, the formidable former linebacker left his guard position and made for the drinks cart. Rachel flipped open the reservoir lid, swiped an arm through melting ice, and pulled out a couple of cold water bottles to hand to Garth. He wiped his brow on his sleeve and thanked her gruffly.

Rachel squinted at Tiffany through the gap in the circle left by Garth's temporary absence. "How is she?"

"Nasty scrape on her forehead. Otherwise she seems to be moving her neck and head okay."

They overheard Wendy ask Derek, "Is there anything in your cart to eat?"

"How can Wendy think about food at a time like this?" Garth blustered. Worry threaded through annoyance. He sprinted to Tiffany's side as if headed for a touchdown.

Rachel filled a plastic cup with water and placed it on the nearby concrete for Mopette. The pet delicately dipped her pink tongue into the cup to taste-test before thirstily lapping the water.

Straightening, Rachel whispered for Mickey's ears alone. "Tiffany eats like a bird. At the buffet this morning she chased down an egg and a solitary blueberry with at least four flutes of champagne and orange juice, and totally ignored her Cobb salad later in the salon when we bridesmaids were getting our hair styled for the wedding." She waved a hand airily. "With this heat—" She left the obvious conclusion unsaid.

"Tiff fainted from low blood sugar?"

"Sure, most likely," Rachel agreed, keeping to herself the speculation that if *she* managed to hide a smartphone in her own lavish bouquet, Tiffany had the opportunity to conceal a flask of alcohol in hers.

A commotion at the hotel distracted their attention from the injured bridesmaid. A small group started across the lawn to the Rockery. Although still too far away to identify without her glasses, she surmised the paramedics had arrived.

"The ambulance must have been in the vicinity to get here so fast," Rachel observed. "What luck." That, or the GM had prepared for all eventualities on this important weekend.

In short order a lone police constable and two paramedics assumed control. Tiffany vehemently refused to be loaded onto a stretcher and taken to hospital. "It's mild heat exhaustion," she was overheard to insist. "I'll be fine."

The constable took down names for his report, chatted briefly with the panting GM who'd chased him across the lawn from the parking lot, and left.

The paramedics checked Tiffany's blood pressure and temperature, palpated for broken bones, and cleaned and bandaged the superficial scrape on her forehead. Then they questioned her closely about what she'd eaten and drunk that day. They insisted she drink an entire bottle of water. One paramedic watched while Tiffany swallowed a few bites of an energy bar. The other treated bloody scratches on Raynald's face and hands.

Finally satisfied that Tiffany did not exhibit signs of heatstroke or a concussion, and after Garth promised to keep a close eye on her for twenty-four hours, they allowed Garth to swing her up into tree-trunk arms and convey her to the hotel to rest in her room.

The senior paramedic shook Wendy's hand and spoke for a minute or two to Halden and Asta. Rachel overheard the phrases "shower to cool her down," "no alcohol," and "get some food in her stomach."

A small armada of electric golf carts crested the hotel parking lot curb and rolled down the grassy slope past the tennis courts to the Rockery. One split off and aimed for Garth's tall bulk striding across the lawn to the hotel with Tiffany in his arms. When several other two-seater carts pulled up, Halden escorted Candy over to the nearest one. Rachel recognized the Australian golf pro at the wheel. After the two men carefully arranged the trailing gown to Candy's satisfaction, Halden climbed into a cart driven by the GM. In parallel the carts zoomed off to the hotel.

The show over, Wendy and the guests approached the remaining golf carts for a ride or took the beachside path to the hotel. The photographer and his assistant loaded camera equipment into the last remaining golf cart. Derek folded shade umbrellas and collected discarded drinks.

The wedding planner collapsed into a Muskoka chair and rubbed her temples. "I'm ruined," she was overheard to whine. "No one in LA will ever hire me again."

Mickey transferred Mopette's leash to Rachel and wandered over to the granite slope to retrieve the formal morning coat he'd tossed aside during the emergency. After a few halfhearted swipes at the dust and creases, he slung the crumpled jacket over a shoulder.

"Candy is going to kill Tiffany," Mickey predicted as he rejoined Rachel on the lawn. They shared a grimace.

Rachel automatically offered, "Give the jacket to me, and I'll clean it before the banquet."

"Holy Rental Deposit." Mickey batted away the outstretched hand. "No way, Rach. The concierge will arrange for professional dry cleaning." He gestured at the stained jacket on the concrete marking the location where Tiffany had collapsed. "Garth's jacket needs an expert's attention as well. I'll drop them off in the lobby and then let's get a drink in the bar. I sure need one."

"Sure." Private time with Mickey. Her pulse leaped.

Then she recalled that she'd never given him an answer in regards to "exploring a relationship" after the wedding weekend. She rather hoped the shocking incident drove it from his mind. Less pressure that way. Less guilt.

Mickey glanced at his wristwatch. "The banquet starts in less than an hour. Unless it's put off." He noticed her bare feet. "Where are your shoes?"

"My shoes?" Confused, Rachel followed the direction of his gaze to her grass-stained blistered toes. She'd completely forgotten the lavender pumps in the commotion. "I think I ditched them over by the chairs." Then her heart catapulted to her throat. "Oh my gods! My bouquet!" She flapped the hand without the leash in instant panic mode.

While Mickey bundled up Garth's jacket and searched the grass around the white Muskoka chairs for the discarded shoes, she skipped in bare feet across the scorching concrete surface to the granite slab where she'd placed the bouquet with her phone hidden deep inside. Mopette, attached to the leash wrapped around her wrist, trotted at her heels.

Rachel squinted at the dozens of potted flowers and greenery decorating the expanse of sloping granite, her pathetic vision blurry from too much sun, adrenaline, and excitement. Each pot appeared indistinguishable from a bouquet.

"Which one is it?" She hopped from foot to foot. "Ah, ow. It burns," she squealed. Mopette rose on her hind legs, bounced along with Rachel, and barked happily at this new game.

An idea penetrated Rachel's desperation. "Mopette, did Candy teach you doggy tricks? Can you fetch? Fetch bouquet."

Mopette plunked her rear down, waved her front paws at Rachel, and yipped.

"I said *fetch*, not sit."

Mopette barked twice. Her beady black eyes and cocked head conveyed a doggy message only a dog owner might understand.

"You want me to pick you up? Are your paws too hot?" Rachel bent to comply. Her reaching arms paused in midair when she noticed the wet stream darkening the rock under Mopette's tush.

"Ha-ha! You didn't pee on me *this* time, you incontinent little rascal!" Rachel backed away, swishing her chiffon skirt with her free hand.

Belatedly aware that Mickey witnessed her odd behavior, Rachel tossed the end of the leash in his direction. "Please escort Mopette to the lawn. She has unfinished business. And so do I."

Without waiting for his reply, Rachel pranced on tiptoes the length of the outlook, pausing to scrutinize every decorative flowerpot. "Oh my gods," she muttered to no one in particular. "What could have happened? A bouquet doesn't simply get up and walk away."

A freshening breeze from the east carried the sound of Mopette's proud "yip-yip" from under the trees. Rachel lurched to a halt. A dreadful idea bloomed. *Nah*, Mopette couldn't possibly have had anything to do with the bouquet's disappearance. The little dog's mouth was too small to fit around the wrapped flower stems.

Then Rachel remembered the lavender satin ribbons dangling from those wrapped stems.

Oh nooooooooooo. Bad dog!

Chapter 15

The Bouquet Hunter

Half an hour later, the wedding planner tracked down the three groomsmen and two bridesmaids in the hotel's air-conditioned rustic bar, where they'd settled gratefully into deep leather chairs. Half-empty glasses of water and beer dotted the surface of a slate-topped coffee table.

The frazzled middle-aged woman's mauve cap-sleeved dress badly needed ironing. She collapsed into a chair, the day's strain evident in thin pinched lips and rosy slashes of freshly applied blush that flamed incongruously on pale skin. Rachel learned her name was Veronique—surely a fake French name for a woman with a thick Boston accent. A female server scurried over to take her drink order.

Veronique asked about Tiffany's health. Garth sat slumped, sleeves rolled up, morosely staring into the distance. He roused himself to mutter, "Tiffany kicked me out of her room." Rachel felt for him, poor guy. Worrying about the girl sucked the life out of him.

Avoiding that sore subject, Veronique proceeded to relay Halden's instructions. The wedding banquet had been rescheduled for nine o'clock to accommodate indoor photos of the bride and groom with their relatives, and to give the bride's medication sufficient time to resolve a splitting headache. She swiped at her phone screen and then read off the salon appointments for each member of the wedding party to have their hair washed and styled and, in the bridesmaids' case, makeup freshened for the evening's festivities. Tiffany was not expected to attend. She reminded the men to drop off their sweat-drenched clothing to the concierge in the lobby for one-hour dry-cleaning service.

"One last thing regarding the family group photos," Veronique said. "The bride's bouquet is, ah—"

"History?" Wade interjected.

"Pulverized?" Mickey offered. Asta stretched out a tanned arm to give his shoulder a warning push.

Veronique's sharp eyes skewered Wade and Mickey. "I was going to say *unavailable*." She shook her head, straight bleached white hair swishing across her shoulders. "The bride's unfortunate, ah—"

Wade raised his brows. "Meltdown?"

"Candy went berserk," Mickey corrected easily. "She flayed that photographer with her bouquet like a madwoman. Never saw anything like it, onscreen or off." Then he yelped in pain and swore.

Garth raised his head. "What gives?"

Mickey pointed an accusing forefinger at Garth's sister. "Asta kicked me!"

"You deserved it," he gloomily rumbled. "No matter how outrageous Candy's behavior, that's our sister-in-law you're trashing. She's family."

Asta nodded, grim furrows between her fair brows. "For better or worse."

Veronique sniffed in agreement and peered over reading glasses at Mickey. "Really, Mr. McNichol. That was uncalled for." She waved mauve-tipped fingers in the air vaguely.

"Stress. The excitement. These things happen." Then she remembered the task at hand. "Let's move on. Bottom line, the bride needs a replacement bouquet for the family photos and to toss after the banquet."

Rachel recoiled deep into the leather chair, willing herself invisible. No such luck. Veronique's questioning tilt of the head targeted her. "I've lost mine," Rachel reluctantly admitted.

"Lost?" The frosty response chilled Rachel more than the cool air from an overhead vent. "How on *earth* did you lose a three hundred dollar bouquet?"

Rachel squirmed. Her gaze fastened on the hands clenched in her lap. *Three hundred dollars. Yikes.* She hoped the wedding planner didn't make her pay for a replacement. "The dog must have snatched it during the chaos after Tiffany—"

"Passed out," said Mickey and Wade simultaneously.

"I resent that." Garth's big blond head and muscular upper body swung upright like those of an angry polar bear. "Tiff fainted from the heat and lack of food."

Wade and Mickey exchanged glances. Under his breath Wade murmured, "Denial ain't just a river in Egypt." Mickey rolled his eyes.

"You boys are terrible." Asta rose in a fluid motion from her chair and fluffed out creases in the skirt's yards of chiffon. "After Garth carried Tiffany back to the hotel, I collected Tiffany's bouquet. I asked the staff to store it in the kitchen cooler along with my bouquet. I'll fetch one immediately for Candy to use this evening. Problem solved."

Hope swelled Rachel's chest. "Asta, did you pick up my bouquet rather than Tiffany's?" That would explain its disappearance. She jumped to her feet, ready to race Asta to the cooler. She knew a shortcut to the kitchen via a service corridor.

Asta hesitated before replying. She nodded at the wedding planner. “Thank you, Veronique.”

The wedding planner took the hint and her glass of iced tea, and departed.

After the woman disappeared through the bar door into the lobby, Asta continued. “In answer to your question, Rachel, unless *you* hid three minibar bottles of vodka in your bouquet, I’m assuming it was Tiffany’s.”

Air whooshed out of Garth’s lungs as if a football had slammed into his gut at fifty miles per hour. Asta’s eyes softened. She placed a compassionate hand on her brother’s massive shoulder. “Empties fell out when I picked it up. Sorry, big brother.”

Rachel’s shoulders slumped. She could *not* catch a break this weekend.

Asta targeted Wade and Mickey with a wagging forefinger. “Gentlemen, be kind. What I said goes no further than this room.”

Garth pushed his hands up and through his dark blond hair, scowling fiercely at the beer glasses on the small table as if the universal availability of alcohol were to blame for Tiffany’s addiction.

Asta bent to console him. “It’s a disease. Tiff requires professional help to beat this,” she said, patting Garth’s mussed hair into place. “There’s nothing you can do.”

“We’ll see about that. Work will fix her up. There’s nothing like sixteen-hour days on location to kick a bad habit.” Garth reached to robustly slap Mickey on the back, almost knocking him off his chair. “Right, old buddy?” To the others he explained, “Mickey is going to sign Tiffany, keep her too busy acting to drink.”

Mickey froze under the group's scrutiny like a Muskoka deer caught in headlights.

Asta shrugged tanned shoulders. She'd said her piece. "Catch you in the spa salon in half an hour for our appointment, Rach."

Rachel saw an opening. She also had a bouquet to retrieve, namely her own. She murmured an excuse, pleading the desire for a long, cool shower.

Following Asta out of the bar, Rachel paused to snag a frosty bottle of sparking water from Derek's laden tray. "How's the chef's temper?" she whispered to her tall friend, thinking of the meals for over one hundred guests that the kitchen crew had to set back to nine o'clock.

Derek chuckled. "Ricardo? He's swearing up a storm, threatening to quit. The staff's happy about the overtime, though." He paused. A flush swept up his neck to redden his face. "Hey, Rachel, I've been thinking about, ah, getting together. What do ya say?"

"To go jogging?"

"Not *jogging*," he said with contempt. He cleared his throat and looked up at the ceiling, over her shoulder, anywhere but at her while he gathered courage. "Like a *date*. I'll even buy."

"Oh." One day dolled up like the celebrity guests, and he gets interested in *that* way. *Sheesh.* Rachel didn't have a minute to ponder how to deal with this latest complication. "Up to now you've never even offered to buy me a popsicle in Port Carson!"

Embarrassed, he stepped backward. "You're out of my league. I get it."

"Out of your league? I'm a *chambermaid*." Astonished, she attempted to put him straight. "Derek, this isn't really me." She passed a hand down her front to indicate her hair, expensive dress, and matching heels. "It's a costume. Tomorrow I'll be back in uniform." She forced a laugh. "When I'm my regular self again, you'll feel differently."

"No, I won't." He regarded her with love-sick cow eyes.

She bit her lip in consternation. The only man in her heart had Hollywood written all over him. "Buddy, I gotta dash. We'll go jogging on Tuesday. Talk then."

Straddling the line between the worlds of hotel guests and staff members sure was getting complicated. Besides, to quote Yogi Berra, "It ain't over till it's over." Thrusting Derek's newfound interest out of her mind, she dashed barefoot through the service wing, humming the melody of "I Wanna Be Loved By You." An exciting evening lay ahead at Mickey's side.

And, the gods willing, later in his bed.

★★★★★

In her tiny single room, alone at last, Rachel carefully laid the bridesmaid's dress out flat on the bed. In her underwear she sat cross-legged on the floor and rubbed aloe sunburn lotion onto the bottoms of smarting feet and antibiotic cream on the blisters on her toes.

This bridesmaid gig shook her to the core of her identity in ways she'd never anticipated. Transforming from plain to pretty and consequently being pursued by two handsome men was both exciting and confusing. However, there was no point in worrying her dyed head about it. Mickey had a plane ticket home, and she expected Derek's sudden romantic interest to disappear on Sunday along with her fancy dress.

She pulled on some tennis socks to cushion her feet on her little excursion, then rummaged through the dresser drawers for a suitable disguise to wear on the hunt for her bouquet.

The experiences of the past two days had shattered long-held illusions about celebrities' golden, perfect lives. Candy and Tiffany had it all—beauty, fame, talent, wonderful men desperately in love with them—yet behaved so appallingly when it counted. But who was she to judge? She'd barely escaped making the biggest morally degenerate mistake of her life by planning to exploit a genuinely good guy like Halden.

But you didn't betray him, she reassured herself. Tiffany ruined Halden and Candy's day, not her. *After I find my phone and delete those pictures, I can go on with my life guilt-free.* She quickly dressed in a faded navy Muskoka-branded hoodie and baggy yoga pants.

As she tied the laces of her beat-up runners, she stewed over her powerful attraction to Mickey. Oh, how she desperately longed to risk finishing what they started in the lake the previous evening. From his eager kisses in the water and astonishing suggestion that she join him in California, she surmised he shared the same lustful desire, unless...if he discovered she'd taken photos with the intent to sell them, he'd hate her. She must *never* let that happen. The incriminating photos must be deleted, and fast.

Then there was the responsibility she owed her employer. Rachel's good-girl side insisted she obey the hotel's no hook-up rule. But the powerful passion ruling her heart demanded she enjoy every second of a romantic one-night stand with Mickey. Because her decision during the wedding meant she couldn't afford to study to become a cinematographer, in California or anywhere else.

She drew the hood over flaxen hair that glowed like a beacon and grabbed her thick dark-rimmed glasses from the top of the dresser. At *last* she'd be able to see where that furry little scamp had hauled her bouquet. It couldn't have been far. The bouquet weighed half as much as the dog. She checked the time on the bedside alarm clock, calculating she'd have to be back in her room in ten minutes to shower, don her dress, and then report to Marie-Eve in the spa salon for her hair and makeup appointment.

On with the hunt.

★★★★★

With increasing desperation, Rachel scoured every inch of the Rockery, then zipped along the beach and circled the Muskoka chairs under the pines. Nothing. Breathing hard, she approached the gloomy thicket of trees delineating the property boundary. She checked her watch. Only a couple more minutes left.

With the aid of her glasses, she spied the massive German shepherd prowling soundlessly between tall pines thirty feet away. A small child could ride him like a pony. The police service dog ambled at the heels of the female security guard she'd practically run smack into yesterday. The two were obviously on patrol.

Everyone knew police dogs had supersensitive noses and were trained to track humans and locate drugs. Why not a bouquet? After holding it for hours, the wrapped bundle of stems must be well saturated with sweat. Fortunately she hadn't showered yet. Her scent was definitely ripe for the sniffing.

What an incredible stroke of luck to stumble across the police dog and its handler. She'd recruit them in the search. From television police-procedural dramas, she understood how it worked. The dog sniffed an article of clothing with the target's scent, then smelled the air and nosed along the ground until it picked up the airborne or ground track.

Rachel darted across the lawn to within ten feet of the statuesque uniformed guard and the enormous dog at her hip, its long pink tongue lolling as it panted in the heat. She skidded to a stop on the thick carpet of pine needles.

"Hey there."

The guard, natural brown curls loose about her shoulders, halted, swiveled. "Hey yourself. Your toy dog's not with you today?"

Rachel froze, forgetting to breathe. "You *recognized* me?"

The other woman snickered. "Sure do. Were you trying for incognito with those ugly glasses and hoodie? That only works on TV."

Rachel didn't have time to bemoan the inadequacy of her disguise. She needed that bouquet found. After checking that the guard had the dog's leash firmly grasped in her left hand, Rachel inched up to a conversational distance. "I'm sorry, I've forgotten your name."

A sympathetic smile lit the woman's neutral expression. "No wonder. You were scared yesterday, along with your dog. I'm Catrina Turner." She laid a hand on the dark beast's head in the vast space between two alertly pointed ears. "And this is Titan."

The beast opened mighty jaws and barked twice. The air vibrated with a sound wave that slammed into Rachel like a physical force. She fought to contain a scream. "Hooo, boy. Now that I see Titan up close, *I* almost peed."

"Titan usually inspires that reaction." Catrina remained unperturbed. "What can I do for you?"

"Here's the thing." Rachel got to the point, the words tumbling out breathlessly fast in sync with her racing heartbeat. "Mopette—that's the dog—dragged my bridesmaid's bouquet somewhere, and I can't find it. Is it possible for Titan to locate it for me? I have to dress for the wedding banquet."

"Why not?" Catrina said. "You'll have to come closer. Let him sniff you."

"I know that." Still Rachel hesitated. What big teeth he had. Wolf-sharp.

Gulping, Rachel advanced within range of the dog's snout, leaned forward, and gingerly presented a sacrificial left forearm and balled fist. She squeezed her eyes closed and prayed. A moist nose swiped her skin. Startled, she jerked back, lost her balance, and landed on her tush.

Catrina chortled. "Titan won't bite. Unless I issue the command," she qualified. "You're perfectly safe." She motioned to Rachel's feet. "Give me one of your footies. That should do it."

Rachel tugged off a running shoe and tennis sock. "It's coated inside with aloe lotion and antibiotic cream," she said, tossing the scrap of cloth at the dog's front paws. The dog lowered his head to nudge the material with his snout. "Won't the multiple smells confuse him?"

"Not a problem. German shepherds are able to distinguish between thousands of scents. He's got a good whiff of you and now the footie. What should I do with the bouquet when he finds it?"

Rachel replaced the shoe, scrambled to her feet, and brushed pine needles and dirt off her rear end. "I've gotta run. Please leave it at Reception for Rachel." She sprinted in the direction of the hotel, yelled over her shoulder, "Thanks so much."

"Hey," Catrina called after her. "I've got Titan. I'm not allowed near the hotel with the dog."

But Rachel was well out of earshot. Shrugging her shoulders, Catrina reached down to scratch Titan behind the ears.

Softly she complained, “And I can’t trust you alone out here even for a few minutes, can I, boy? Darn rabbits.”

Chapter 16

Only You

[♫ "I Wanna Be Loved By You"]

"I wanna be loved by you…" Marilyn's seductive voice sashayed through Mickey's mind as he whistled the tune while adjusting his freshly pressed cravat before a large mirror.

Shaved, showered, and presentable once again, he, Wade, Halden, and Garth waited for the bridesmaids in the foyer at the entrance to the dining room. They'd been informed that Candy insisted on a procession to the head table once the majority of the guests were seated, with the bride and groom leading the way. A grim Halden stood off to the side, intently texting on his smartphone.

"You're awfully chipper, Mick," Wade said over Mickey's shoulder to his reflection, "considering it's been a hell of a day so far."

Mickey cocked his head and winked. "I've been thinking about a beautiful bridesmaid."

Garth, big shoulders slumped, lamented, "Yeah, me too. Tiffany still won't let me in her room. She's probably too embarrassed."

Ever cynical, Wade snorted. "Did you manage to empty the restocked minibar in her room before she kicked you out?"

Garth paled under his tan. "No. But she wouldn't—I mean, the paramedic expressly told her no alcohol. I left instructions with room service. Food but no alcohol." He straightened. "I should go check on her."

"Too late." Halden laid a firm restraining hand on Garth's bicep. "Here come my lovely bride and the girls."

★★★★★

Contrary to Asta's dire prediction that Candy'd ordered vegetarian for the wedding banquet, the guests were offered three main course options: fresh linguini with vegetables and pesto sauce; tiny, succulent quail on a bed of wild rice and a side of baby carrots flavored with Canadian maple syrup; or shelled lobster accompanied by asparagus and tiny purple potatoes.

Not that Mickey paid much attention to the meal with Candy's lovely, quirky cousin seated on his left at the head table. He entertained Rachel with Hollywood gossip. She asked intelligent questions about the movie biz. Seriously impressed by her encyclopedic knowledge of films and those who made them, he enjoyed trying to stump her. A woman with that much passion for filmmaking belonged in Hollywood.

And, fingers crossed, in his bed at the end of the evening festivities.

When Garth pushed back his chair beside the bride and stood to assume his master of ceremonies duties, Mickey entwined his fingers with Rachel's. Under his thumb on her wrist, her strong pulse thrummed rapidly. Anticipation, his experience with women suggested. His groin stirred.

The toasts to the bride and groom didn't take long. Asta filled in for the missing maid of honor with a sweet welcome from the Armstrong family for Candy and a toast to her brother's happiness. Glasses clinked. Halden obligingly rose, bent Candy back in a romantic embrace, and soundly kissed his bride.

Garth read his best man's speech off of a couple of crinkled sheets of paper. Mickey, Halden's first talent agent before he jumped to a more prestigious agency, had contributed a humorous anecdote to Garth's speech. Mickey was pleased when Halden chuckled at Garth's retelling of how an early screen test went horribly wrong when the actress kissed Halden and promptly forgot her lines.

Candy, exquisite but paler than usual, had regained her regal composure. Her tinkling laugh rang off key after several guest tributes to Halden's prowess as an actor and producer ignored her completely. The outpouring of warmth from those Halden left behind in Wisconsin and the many new friends he made on his rise to stardom raised the positive energy in the room, lightening Halden's mood.

Mickey surmised he wasn't the only person to realize Halden's guests vastly outnumbered Candy's. Even her own cousin Rachel smiled prettily but had no fond memories to share in public, nor even in private to him. Sad really. He scanned the room for Candy's photographer friend but was unable to discern Raynald's skinny frame among the formally attired male guests. Likely she'd lost *that* friend after thrashing him with her bouquet.

From his vantage point facing the rest of the room, Mickey observed with surprise that tonight Wendy sat at a round table with Wisconsin relatives near the head table instead of at the back of the room. Halden must've ordered the switch in table assignments in appreciation for calmly taking control at the photo session debacle, because sure as hell Candy would *never* have arranged that perk.

In the short time Candy had lived in California, she'd hired and fired two PAs. Come to think of it, maybe they'd quit. The sloe-eyed manner in which Wendy trained big brown eyes on Halden reminded him of how Mopette staked out a tasty treat. Mickey doubted *she'd* be quitting anytime soon.

After the bride's and groom's respective fathers made their toasts and the newlyweds gamely smooched one last time cued by the clinking of glasses, Garth asked Michael Bublé to stand.

"Folks, you all know the Canadian actor, singer, and songwriter Michael Bublé, winner of multiple Grammy and international music awards. We are privileged to have Michael and the backup band entertain us in the ballroom for the rest of the evening. Please join us there for wedding cake and dancing."

★★★★★

The traditional cake-cutting ceremony was staged in the center of the ballroom on a circular wood dance floor, after which the pastry chef rolled the table out of the room. Servers in white shirts, black trousers, and lavender bow ties served samples of lavender-iced wedding cake and beverages to guests at round tables for six arranged in a U-shape around the dance floor. A long table loaded with a selection of rich desserts and a staffed open bar occupied the inside wall opposite a temporary stage.

[♫ "Once in a Lifetime"]

The four-piece band struck up "Once in a Lifetime." Halden escorted his bride onto the dance floor to a smattering of applause. Michael Bublé's smooth croon filled the high-ceilinged room with the glorious love song.

At one of the round tables decorated with lavender-themed flower arrangements and wedding favors, Rachel tugged gently at Mickey's shirt sleeve. He leaned in to hear her over the music.

"Michael Bolton's hit from the 1994 film *Only You*," she whispered.

Candy moved sensuously to the music in Halden's arms. Every man in the room tracked her svelte figure. Mickey pursed his lips and considered the rapier claws she'd kept sheathed until provoked by Raynald that afternoon. Candy's silvery beauty had tarnished, at least in his eyes. Absently he replied. "Didn't it star Hugh Grant?"

Rachel huffed. "Please. Hugh wasn't the only romantic comedy lead back then. Believe it or not, Ironman Robert Downey Jr. starred alongside Marisa Tomei."

Mickey grinned at the intelligent girl at his side. "Bet you don't know who wrote the film score?"

"What do I get in return?"

"A kiss."

"That's it?" Rachel shrugged as if the prize were inconsequential.

His forehead crinkled in feigned surprise, but his heart rate bumped a notch. "You want more than a kiss?"

"Maybe." She fluttered her eyelashes flirtatiously.

Man, she was killing him. "Your wish is my command for the rest of the evening. Will that do?"

"Anything I ask, eh? You're on." Rachel shook his proffered hand. "The film *Only You* was scored by an Academy Award-winning female composer."

"Name?"

She smiled. "A first name *I'll* always remember. Rachel Portman."

"And a first name I'll never forget." Mickey dug into his pocket for his phone to buy the song on the spot for a souvenir of the evening, then remembered the device rested on the bottom of Lake Muskoka. Remembered Rachel's long legs wrapped around him in the cool water. Heat and an aching tension flooded his body. He ditched his jacket and loosened his tie.

[♬ "All of Me"]

The dance came to an end, and the wedding singer introduced the next song, "All of Me." Mickey pulled Rachel to her feet. "Dance with me."

Rachel kicked off her shoes and slipped easily into his arms on the crowded floor. "I'm not familiar with this song."

"That's because it hasn't been in a movie yet," Mickey teased. "This is John Legend's huge hit." He swept her close until her petite but firm breasts pancaked against his chest. Holding one hand, an arm encircling her slim waist, he steered them between couples. The *thump-ka-thump* of her rapid heartbeat synced with his. Rachel's curves and edges fit to the angles of his body as precisely as parts in a German-engineered Porsche.

"I love it," she murmured.

Her cheek nestled against his shoulder. Soft warm breath stirred exposed skin above his shirt collar. The palm of one hand pressed into his back behind his heart as if physically capturing the organ. She'd already captured his heart that afternoon, in the metaphorical sense. The open question that had him stumped was what he intended to do about it.

The prospect of a one-night affair had him more conflicted now than it had the previous evening. Their ardent foreplay in the lake made him uncomfortably aware, in every amorous sense, that even a small taste of Rachel inflamed mind-losing desire. He'd had the urge to stand in front of the pastor with her that afternoon! Sure, he blamed that crazy impulse on heat exhaustion. But by taking her to bed, by going down that rabbit hole, he'd only get in deeper—maybe wouldn't even want to extricate himself. That way lay serious commitment. *Holy Ball and Chain.*

Over Rachel's shoulder he perused the dancing couples, several of them with young kids tucked into bed upstairs. At some point in a man's life an instinctual longing kicked in to settle down, father children, raise the next generation of filmmakers and audiences, and thereby ensure the continuity of the movie biz. That'd explain the magnetic attraction welding his body to the incredible woman in his arms. He'd bedded a dozen gorgeous women, and not one had him contemplating the purchase of an engagement ring. Being immersed in wedding fever among a sea of happy couples had obviously flipped a biological switch.

Would a single long night of energetic sex satiate lust for Candy's cousin nestled against his chest like she belonged there permanently? He needed to find out because if not, he intended to make his suggestion to Rachel to study in California become a reality.

The difficulties occupied his thoughts until Rachel lifted her lips for a soft kiss. His lips eagerly met hers, his mind filled with the singer's dulcet words of everlasting love.

They swayed to love songs, wrapped close, cheek pressed to flushed cheek until the famous singer announced a break for the toss of the wedding bouquet in a few minutes. The two reluctantly separated and returned to their table to discover that the ice had melted in their water glasses. They drained them, then headed to the temporary bar, joining a line behind Halden and Wendy.

Most of the men in the room, Halden included, had removed their jackets, rolled up their sleeves, and made themselves comfortable for a long night of energetic partying. Dark-haired Wendy wore a figure-hugging scarlet number with a plunging neckline that drew the eye to plump breasts—*real* boobs—with a small tattoo of a humpback whale low on the left. It leaped on the swell of her bosom with every indrawn breath.

Surprise, surprise. Candy's competent, dependable PA hid a smoking hourglass figure under the slacks and baggy shirts she habitually wore. For a man who'd tied the knot a few hours earlier, Halden seemed inordinately interested in checking out the scenery. Mickey couldn't avoid overhearing their conversation.

Slightly the worse for wear, Halden braced an elbow on the bar for support, awaiting his order. "I don't know how to thank you for what you did today, Wendy."

Dimples popped in Wendy's cheeks as she smiled up, waaaay up, at Halden. Mickey recognized a flirtatious smile on a woman, and Wendy flashed a classic. His eyes skewed sideways to catch Candy's frowning pout from a nearby table adjacent to the dance floor.

"It was nothing," Wendy asserted with a flip of long brown curls over one bare shoulder. "I lifeguarded at the beach summers during college."

"Like in that nineties *Babewatch* TV series." Halden nodded. "I can definitely see you in one of those swimsuits."

"*Baywatch*," she corrected. And giggled.

Giggled? Uh-oh. She had it bad. And alcohol had loosened Halden's lips disastrously close to the point of inflaming Candy's temper. The bartender placed a double

Scotch whisky, neat, on the polished wood surface by Halden's hand.

Mickey stepped forward and smoothly slid the tumbler along the bar out of Halden's reach. "A large glass of ice water for the groom, my man. Three flutes of champagne for the ladies and one for me."

In short order, Mickey placed a hand between Halden's shoulder blades and propelled him between the tables and chairs to rejoin Candy. Rachel trailed behind carrying a couple of glasses of champagne.

Mickey set the flute he held on the table before Candy. "Here's your drink, beautiful."

"I requested sparkling water, but what the hell. It's my wedding night." Candy tipped the crystal flute to her lips and downed the expensive French champagne in one go. She snapped her fingers. "Hand me another, Mick."

"Sure thing." He nodded to Rachel who set the two flutes she carried on the table before the bride. The alcohol might wash away the petulant irritation marring the perfection of Candy's face.

[♫ "Single Ladies (Put a Ring on It)"]

The DJ cued up Beyoncé's "Single Ladies (Put a Ring on It)." Candy resolutely drained her third glass of expensive bubbly as the wedding planner arrived at their table holding a bridesmaid's bouquet. Veronique efficiently guided Candy to the center of the dance floor and thrust a microphone into Garth's hand.

"Single ladies." Garth's gravelly voice boomed over the catchy tune. "Assemble for the bouquet toss. No age limit. Don't be shy. If you're currently unmarried, step right up. Aunt Margery, that means you."

"That means you, too." Mickey palmed Rachel's delectable butt and gave it a gentle shove in the direction of the dance floor.

"Oh, no," she demurred. "Not me."

"Go on. Candy expects her cousin to be in the photos." He pointed to the official wedding photographer at the ready on the sideline.

Indecision flashed across Rachel's face before she capitulated. "All right then." She padded over in bare feet to join Wendy, Asta, and five guests, including a gray-haired matron in floor-length lime polyester, in the spotlit center of the room. Mickey followed her to the edge of the dance floor for a better view.

"Are you ready, gorgeous ladies?" Garth announced the countdown. "Candy, on three." Candy turned her back to the women and prepared to catapult the bouquet over her head.

"One. Two. Three!"

The bouquet arced high. Wendy leaped like a well-fed gazelle, hooked it out of the air, and waved it triumphantly. Mobile phone and tablet cameras clicked. Cameras flashed.

"That was amazing," Rachel said to Wendy over the music and applause.

"I played softball in high school," Wendy explained. "Right fielder."

Candy stalked their way, a thunderous expression clouding the perfection of her features.

"Wicked witch." Wendy inhaled a fortifying breath and held it.

"Wanda," Candy spat. "What the *hell* do you think you're doing with my bouquet? You're my assistant, not a guest. This is…this is…" A vein bulged beside the left lowered eyebrow as she searched for an appropriate word to express outrage. "You're *fired*."

She dismissed the blanched PA, turned to Rachel, and snarled in a low voice because the song had ended, "And you, *cousin*," arrogant disdain implying Rachel existed lower in the pecking order than a beetle. "How dare you participate in the bouquet toss? You're merely—"

"Who wants to dance?" A familiar voice warbled in the musical lull, cutting short whatever Candy planned to say.

Necks craned to view the speaker at the entrance to the ballroom. Tiffany, beautiful despite mussed blond hair, a bandage on her forehead, and a crumpled bridesmaid's dress, held fast to the door frame.

Conversations ceased. Halden's robust curse echoed in the high-ceilinged space. "Of all the gin joints, in all the world, *she* walks into mine," he groused, misquoting Humphrey Bogart's line in *Casablanca* when Ingrid Bergman shows up in the nightclub.

Candy clamped palms to nonexistent hips, thin arms akimbo—a fierce stance at odds with the delicate femininity she projected on the runway and in the fashion magazines. "Some *idiot* supplied her with booze against my orders," she screeched loud enough for the entire room to hear. "Garth, get that bitch out of here before she ruins this evening too!"

Mickey quickly closed the ten feet between himself and Rachel on the dance floor, and laced her long fingers though his. "That's our cue to exit, kid. We'll give Tiffany's keeper a hand."

Rachel pointed at the best man weaving around tables toward the starlet like a quarterback dodging offensive tackles. "Garth's on it." They watched Garth swing Tiffany up into his arms and carry her out of sight.

Rachel nibbled her bottom lip, lipstick long gone. "Do you think Tiff is plastered? Candy will blame the hotel for supplying her with liquor."

Mickey shrugged. "Tiffany drinks too much, sure, but she's also addicted to attention. She's double trouble."

Mickey wanted to sign a talented rising star to his new agency, not an attention-seeking alcoholic who'd cause nothing but aggravation on set and negative publicity off it. He towed Rachel toward the ballroom entrance. "Let's follow them and find out which it is this time."

On the way he detoured to retrieve his jacket and shrug it on. Rachel slid on her heels, snagged her bag of wedding favors, and stuck it down her bodice where he'd earlier noticed the room key card she carried everywhere peeking over the top of the fabric. Lucky bag. Lucky card.

They caught up with Garth and Tiffany at the lobby elevator. Tiffany sobbed brokenly into the crook of Garth's thick neck. "I need a drink, baby. Only one. Take me to the bar, honey. Please. I'll—I'll do anything you want."

Garth's Nordic blue eyes glistened above the golden curve of her head. "I'm gonna help Tiff beat this, Mick. I'll pay for a month in a residential addiction facility up here in Canada. The studio making the Bond picture will never find out what went down today."

Mickey gripped Garth's shirt-sleeved shoulder. "You're a real hero, my friend. But if you think word won't get back to studio execs and casting directors in California, think again. She's not signed to the picture yet." He thumbed in the direction of the ballroom studded with film stars and waitstaff. "A dozen witnesses are probably tweeting the news this very minute."

"You're a cynic, Mick. Halden's friends and family are loyal. I happen to know the hotel staff signed confidentiality agreements. If anything leaks, I'll see to it that the person responsible is fired."

Rachel emitted a horrified squeak. "But C-Candy doesn't have too many friends in that room."

Garth thrust forward a determined lantern jaw. "Tiffany has friends."

Mickey bit back the brutal truth on the tip of his tongue. Despite her acknowledged talent, unless the starlet cleaned up her act, neither Garth nor any other friend had the power to protect Tiffany from the consequences of her behavior in public and on set. Instead he reached out. "Anything I can do to help her recover, you know I've got your back."

"Sure." Garth frowned impatiently at the static number above the elevator doors. "There are only three floors in this inn. What's taking so long?"

Mickey threw an arm around Rachel's shoulders and drew her alongside for moral support. Although he sympathized with Garth's big-hearted intention to sober Tiffany up, placing her on a big budget film set before she conquered her addiction risked irrevocable damage to her reputation and career.

His gut insisted that he make a difficult decision based on practical realities, not loyalty to his friend. Though he was well aware that by doing so, he'd antagonize a powerful producer. Hollywood was built on relationships. He crossed his fingers that Garth would thank him for what he was about to do.

Eventually.

"Buddy, there's one caveat." From the inside pocket of his jacket Mickey extracted the contract he'd carefully dried with a hair dryer after its dunking in the lake the previous night.

His throat thickened. Breaking bad news was never easy, at least not for him. Making himself heard over Tiffany's pitiful entreaties to be lowered to the floor, he said, "Just so you know, I won't be signing Tiffany York after all. She's in no shape to withstand the pressure of a Bond-girl role."

"What the hell, Mick?" Garth exploded.

At his outburst, Tiffany stilled in Garth's arms. "Bond girl?" she slurred. "That's me."

"Not after your behavior today," Mickey predicted under his breath. He released Rachel to fiercely rip the sheaf of paper crosswise and lengthwise. The fragments fluttered to the bottom of a trash basket.

As if on cue, the elevator doors slid apart. Garth stepped inside with his burden.

"Tiff will prove you wrong," Garth thundered. "I'll remember this. You'll pay—" The closing doors cut off his threat.

Chapter 17

Sleepless in Muskoka

"That went well." Mickey slammed a palm against the polished brass elevator doors.

Rachel's heart squeezed in sympathy. She tentatively laid a consoling hand on his strong back. "Garth will come around. He's desperately in love. Eventually he'll listen to reason. It's obvious to the rest of us that Tiffany will create chaos on any film set until she dries out."

He turned to face her. "As it stands, he's hell-bent on finding out the hard way," he predicted with a sorrowful droop to his fine mouth. "Tiff's manager and my boss at Herron Talent Agency will move heaven and earth to put her in the picture."

A gaggle of chattering guests exited the ballroom and approached the elevator. The party seemed to be breaking up. "Let's discuss this in private." Stiff with repressed agitation, Mickey stalked along the corridor to his room a few doors past the elevator.

Rachel hesitated for a fraction of a second to scan the area for staff witnesses before throwing caution to the wind. Mickey needed comforting, and she was on it like a hot dog on a grill. *Ssssst.* Sizzle, sizzle.

Mickey slid his key card into the slot and held the door for her to enter. The evening chambermaid had drawn the curtains and turned down the summer-weight duvet on the king-sized bed. Soft pools of light from the lamps on the night tables illuminated the stage for a romantic tryst. But Mickey threw his jacket over a chair, sat on the end of the bed, and slumped forward, dark head bowed over knees.

Rachel kicked off the instruments of torture, perched beside him, and sidled close until their shoulders brushed. "If it's the right decision, why are you upset?"

He paused, as if debating internally whether to confide in her, a relative stranger. She draped a consoling arm across his shoulders, and he leaned in, sighed.

In a voice rough with emotion, he finally replied, "In my opinion, Tiffany's only hope is to find the courage to face her demons and save herself. Garth believes *he* can rescue her, like some medieval knight in shining armor. Too bad my decision apparently cost me a friend."

From her observation that weekend, Mickey had a long-term relationship with the Armstrong men solid enough to weather a tiff about Tiff. There had to be more explanation for his distress. "Meanwhile..." she encouraged.

"Meanwhile I don't have the star power signed to be able to afford the lease on an office suite for my own talent agency. The deadline is Monday."

"So the downside is that you can't launch your agency yet? Isn't Hollywood overrun with talented starlets? There'll be other actors and other vacant offices for rent."

He stared at the carpet, unconvinced that his agency had a future.

She recalled the harsh words exchanged at the elevator. "You're worried about your friendship with Garth," she intuited. "He's been your friend forever and is clearly a super-intelligent guy. Due to all the messy wedding drama, he's not thinking straight. He'll figure out what's best for Tiffany."

At that Mickey rallied, straightened, and hugged her close. "You're right. Pheromones addled his brain, that's all," he said into her hair. "I'm being an idiot." He attempted a chuckle.

"He'll come to his senses and realize your intent is to protect Tiffany's career. *I* believe you made the right choice."

Rachel was a practical girl. She of all people understood a decision, either way, had consequences for the other party. Selling photos to the media was right for her career but would've resulted in hurting Halden and his family. *Not* selling them derailed her chance for a Hollywood career. That being said, ethically she'd made the correct decision and could sleep at night. Ditto for Mickey.

However, she had no intention of letting him sleep just yet. Mickey needed a distraction from his problems, and she needed, well…Mickey. Tomorrow she'd return to scrubbing floors. Tomorrow he'd fly home to Tinseltown.

Tonight was theirs.

Her bare feet sank into the thick wool carpet as she padded over to the door to securely lock it. "Earlier you promised that my wish is your command for the rest of the evening. *This* is the rest of the evening."

His lips quirked. "And what is your command, milady?"

It'd been a tough day, for both of them. The hormone buzz from dancing close combined with the stresses of the day begged for release. And she had one surefire stress-busting activity in mind. Heat suffused her cheeks. Never in the years of cleaning rooms had she been tempted to so much as nudge a toe against the line separating the staff from the wealthy guests.

Until now.

In the staff dining room they'd call her nuts to risk her job, heartache, *everything* for one night of sex with this handsome Hollywood agent so out of her league.

She didn't care. She had a heart filled to bursting with stardust passion for Mickey.

One night.

Rachel wedged her legs between his spread knees and began to unbutton his formal striped vest. "You. Me." She angled her head at the vast bed. "In there."

Mickey's dark eyes lit up. "I thought you'd never ask." He stood. His arms circled her ribcage, coaxing her pelvis to contact his. A bulge confirmed his interest.

"Normally I'm not this bold," she admitted. "But time isn't my ally." Her shift began at eight the next morning, leaving only nine hours to spend with Mickey. Precious hours that had to sustain her for the rest of her life. When the panels of the vest swung apart, she tackled the shirt buttons.

Mickey slid his hands down her hips and around to grip her butt. He bent to press urgent lips on hers. His rapid breaths cooled her cheeks as he murmured, "I intend to demonstrate how I feel about you. It'll take hours." He dropped feathery kisses along her chin and down the side of her neck. He thumbed a nipple through chiffon fabric, sending a delicious tingle to her center.

"Promises." She laughed, familiar with men's exaggerated assurances of sexual prowess. She held no expectations, merely coveted the intimacy of being together, of pleasing him.

Her two former boyfriends zipped around the bases in no time flat before sliding home. In fifteen minutes they were done, her own occasional orgasm a pleasant but rare bonus. On the nights she slept over at their apartments, one always fell asleep immediately. The other propped himself up on pillows and watched *Saturday Night Live* or his favorite late-night talk shows. She may as well have been invisible. She'd dated each man for several months before breaking up, vaguely dissatisfied, irrationally wanting to be *important* to a man. And yet who was she?

A nobody.

Mickey pulled the zipper down the back of her dress. The fabric slid down her body, exposing her oh-so-small breasts to the conditioned air. She shivered. Her nipples budded.

Go big or go home.

Rachel slipped off her panties, squeezed her eyelids tight, and boldly offered Mickey a frontal view of her nude body in the flattering glow of bedside lamps.

Noisy breathing signaled activity. She opened one eye to see if he'd reached for the TV remote.

"You are *so* beautiful. Give me a second." Without taking his eyes off her, Mickey slung his belt onto the deep armchair, followed by his vest, shirt, trousers, and socks. "I'll be right there. Don't move." Clad only in boxers, Mickey hastened over to a metal suitcase open on a luggage stand and rummaged in it for condoms.

A bundle of nerves, Rachel folded her discarded clothing and piled on top her master key card and the French-lace wedding favor bag filled with mints that had fallen out of the bodice.

She tugged smooth the thin duvet and was nervously fluffing a down pillow when Mickey threw a handful of condom packages on the night table, wrapped muscled forearms around her waist, and nuzzled the back of her neck. "You do that like a pro."

Little do you know!

She swiveled in the circle of his arms and flattened callused palms on firm pecs. Dark hair tickled her fingers. His heart drummed vigorously under warm skin. "Mick, I'm nervous. I've never done anything like this before."

He put a slight distance between them to stare into her eyes with consternation. "You're a virgin?"

She choked. "Oh, no. That's not what I meant to say." She struggled for the right words, finally blurting the truth. "I've never had a one-night stand in a hotel room."

"The way I see it, one night won't be enough. Unfortunately I have a plane to catch tomorrow afternoon." His mouth twisted in a rueful grimace.

The verbal acknowledgment of his departure arrowed her heart. *I'm wasting precious minutes.* She thrust her hands against tight six-pack abs and toppled them both onto the bed. "Show me how a Hollywood agent from Wisconsin makes love."

"Are you sure?" he mumbled against her lips.

In answer, she slid one hand inside his boxer shorts. As her fingers encircled the thick, rigid proof that he wanted her, warmth pooled in her tingling girl parts. *Eros, God of Love!* "*So* sure."

Outside thunder rumbled far down Lake Muskoka.

Mickey flipped her on her back, nudged one thigh between hers. Resting on one forearm, he explored her body with gentle sweeps of a free hand. Softly, slowly, as if caressing a precious object and not her skinny frame, his lips and fingers stroked her skin for endless minutes. Sensitivity built, every drifting movement over nerve endings contributing to the urgency pooling in her breasts and groin.

Her fingers reached for his throbbing member, so granite hard. So ready for her. She attempted to shift to accommodate him.

He pressed her back into the soft bedding. "Not yet." Pinning her arms to the bed, he lowered his mouth to her inner folds.

Oh my gods! She'd read about men who did the woman first but believed it never happened in real life. Then her mind blanked at the delicate touch of a firm, wet tongue on her engorged nub. His tongue lapped, and her back involuntarily arched.

Can this be happening to me?

Then he thrust his firm, thick tongue straight down her tunnel of love, sliding, retreating, licking the swollen nub, squeezing her butt with strong fingers to align her pelvis for better access. Her breasts pointed to the heavens. Her hands flattened the pristine duvet.

Every flick of his tongue ramped up the sensations in her wiring. Never, ever had she been so…so charged. So desperate to feel a man plunge inside.

She writhed on the king bed. Her boneless limbs flung spread-eagled, fingers scrunching the eight-hundred-thread-count duvet cover into a thousand wrinkles. Nothing existed but the divine sensations surging through her body.

"Mickey, I want you. *Now.*"

He ignored her pleas, his busy tongue fondling the C-spot, circling the nub with agonizingly deliberate movements, taking his time. His finger found the G-spot she'd only ever read about. *Gods almighty*, this guy'd mastered the entire alphabet.

Exquisite pressure built Mount Vesuvius high.

Thunder rolled in from the lake, drowning her rapturous cries. "I'm gonna burst into a million pieces. Get inside me quick," she begged.

He came up to breathe, then dove back inside, thrusting, licking, sucking, purposely driving her to the outer limits with need.

A final synchronized expert flick of tongue and finger ignited a release that convulsed her entire body in wave after wave of incandescent ecstasy. A stupendous crack of lightning swallowed her scream.

Mickey held her tight in his arms while her entire being shuddered, trembled with aftershocks. During the crashing thunder that followed the lightning strike, she imagined she heard Mickey whisper he loved her. *Nah*, her mind must be playing tricks.

Her blown mind.

"Oh my gods, Mickey. My circuits are fried. I can't move."

He merely laughed.

After an eternity, strength ebbed into limp limbs. "It's your turn, Mick."

He smoothed strands of hair from her damp forehead and kissed her cheek. "You're not ready, sweetheart. We have all night."

In that instant Rachel tumbled helplessly, hopelessly in love.

★★★★★

Mopette! Rachel awoke from a nightmare featuring the tiny white dog dangling from a monstrous hound's jaws. She sat up abruptly, displacing the arm Mickey'd flung across her chest.

"What's wrong?" Mickey mumbled. He pried open an eyelid to peer at the illuminated bedside clock. "It's two in the morning."

"Wendy was supposed to walk Mopette before bedtime."

"So?" Mickey groped for the closest breast. "Com'ere, beautiful."

She ignored him and reached to push the wall switch for the bedside lamps. "Candy fired Wendy after the bouquet toss."

Blinking in the light, Mickey levered himself up on elbows. "I saw that coming."

"The poor, neglected pet." Rachel threw off the duvet and began to climb out of bed.

"What? Hold on a second. Where're you going?" He reached to scoop her waist. "You can't bust into the Bridal Suite at this hour. Candy took Mopette for her evening constitutional or, more likely, ordered someone to do it. It's her dog."

Rachel sagged against him. "You're right, of course. I woke up in a panic."

Mickey licked his forefinger, then reached and rubbed an ultrasensitive nipple oh so slowly. Her girl parts clenched, instantly wet. He had her buttons down.

"I have an idea how to relax you."

Rachel raised a questioning brow. "I'm listening."

"Shower massage jets."

★★★★★

An hour later, they tumbled exhausted and sated onto the bed. Pulsing hot water jets on three walls of the double shower had pummeled their bodies during frantic lovemaking. Mickey, his mouth fastened to hers, demonstrated creative uses for a small curved bar of soap. No wonder so many hotel soaps disappeared into guests' luggage.

Mickey began to snore softly, his naked body splayed facedown in the center of the mattress. Tenderly she drew a sheet over him, switched off the lamps, and crawled in beside him.

[♫ "Nobody Does It Better"]

She closed her eyes, floated in a bubble of happiness, and ran fingers through Mickey's thick head of hair. Four orgasms in *one* night.

Not in one *month*.

One *night*.

She lusted after Mick's body, sure. But she *loved* his character—the considerate caring, cynical wit, casual confidence. He said out loud what she'd never *dare* say. His integrity influenced her to be a better person.

That weekend she'd discovered that the actors she'd put on a pedestal for so many years were regular people with normal problems. The photo-shoot debacle had dumped cold water on her burning desire to work on Hollywood film sets to be near them.

She still wanted to move to California, but for a different reason—to be with Mickey. However, he lived in a world of fakery, and truthfully she herself was a fake above all fakes. Did *she* deserve *him*? Suddenly wide awake, she sat up and absently nibbled the edge of a manicured thumbnail.

Before he fell asleep, he'd suggested they exchange contact information at breakfast. He'd ordered room service while she was in the bathroom. She'd truthfully explained that breakfast was impossible. Duty compelled her to leave early. Was it her fault that he'd assumed the duty involved walking Mopette?

Lunch then, he'd insisted. She mentally calculated the time necessary to turn over her allotment of rooms by the three o'clock check-in. Even an hour break for a meal in town was impossible to fit in. Or so she told herself.

Besides, she'd promised Candy to keep her true status a secret. If Mickey ever discovered he'd slept with a hotel chambermaid rather than Candy's cousin, he'd be aghast at the deception. It's a simple matter to cut and run when the girl lives three thousand miles away from your own home.

Mickey turned on his side. In his sleep, his arm curled around her waist to draw her to him. He nestled against the length of her body. "Rachel," he mumbled.

She brushed a forelock of dark hair from his forehead and released a shuddering breath over the lump in her throat. Her heart ached at the thought of never seeing him again. *I can't bear to lose him.*

A plan germinated. Why not reinvent herself, actually *become* the person he believed her to be?

"You have my heart, Mickey. Take care of it until I save enough money to fly out to Hollywood."

Chapter 18

As Bad as It Gets

Taps on the solid wood door woke Mickey. A ray of sun lasered through a narrow gap in the window curtains, hitting him in the eyes. He yawned, stretched, and rolled over to kiss Rachel.

No Rachel.

"Argggh!" He pressed one hand on cool sheets where her body had lain. No morning sex, then, either. She'd given him a heads-up that duty called in the morning, yet disappointment gnawed. At this moment she was probably walking Mopette.

Insistent knocks on the thick door reminded him that he'd ordered room service. He confirmed the time on the bedside clock radio. Eight o'clock. He rolled out of bed and shrugged on Rachel's discarded bathrobe. A heaviness settled in his heart. He missed her. At this moment he craved her presence more than coffee, which he desperately needed to clear a tired brain.

He opened the door wide to allow the room service attendant to carry a tray into the room, and plucked his discarded trousers from the armchair to extract a bill from his wallet for the tip.

What a night. He'd snatched maybe three hours sleep total. He grinned like a fool at the memory of Rachel's passionate antics in the wee hours. She gave as good as she got. His stomach growled, demanding fuel after the hours of energetic sex. The attendant pocketed the tip with a grateful nod, swept the curtains wide to eye-squinting morning sunshine, and withdrew.

To fill the lonely silence, Mickey pressed the television remote and flipped channels until he landed on an American Sunday morning show. Coffee in hand, he propped Rachel's pillows on top of his own and reclined on the bed to watch.

One minute into the show, a familiar image had Mickey lurching to his knees, coffee sloshing onto the bedding. "No frigging way!" he yelped.

On the wall-mounted forty-inch flat screen, in a close-up as large as life, tears glistened on Halden's cheeks as he gazed adoringly at his bride's upturned face. Mickey cursed the photographer who'd managed to evade security and snap an intimate wedding photo. Consternation flashed into fury. How dare he invade that private moment during the ceremony and parade it for the world to gawk at!

Then it got worse. A veritable wedding album of photo stills scrolled across the screen. Given the angles, only a person actually *at* the wedding could have snapped those shots and leaked them to the media. One of Halden's own guests betrayed him!

His heart slamming his chest, Mickey watched the segment until the end in case the scumbag had scored pics of Candy's public meltdowns at the photo-shoot and wedding reception. When the image of a different celebrity flashed onscreen and the hostess moved on, Mickey released the breath he hadn't realized he held. If Candy's inappropriate behavior had been broadcast, Halden's humiliation would've been cruelly magnified.

He reached for the landline to call Halden, then paused. Given the speed that news spread via social media, that photo of the emotionally vulnerable "superhero" had already been shared around the world.

Cursing under his breath, he scrambled to unplug his tablet from the desk charging station. In seconds he launched the Twitter app. Trending derogatory hashtags—#ApolloBreakdown, #SuperWuss, and #ManofMush—had him grinding his teeth.

Due to the three-hour time difference, most Californians were still asleep. There was a chance for damage control on the West Coast. Wade was a lawyer and had connections. Then reason penetrated seething anger. He already knew what Wade's response would be, damn it: accept that the voracious entertainment media had already sunk its teeth deep into this story, rendering legal efforts to suppress the pictures a futile waste of time and money.

Tossing that strategy aside, he contemplated how best to distract Halden to allow him to enjoy his first day as a married man and remain blissfully unaware of the embarrassing leak for as long as possible.

By prior arrangement, Halden expected Mickey, Garth, and Wade to join him for a quick nine holes at a ten o'clock tee-off. Halden knew Mickey too well and would question his roiling internal rage. He'd be wise to burn it off before he met up with the guys. He decided to go for a run, hoping he'd encounter Rachel with Mopette. Being with her always raised his spirits.

★★★★★

Warm sun promised another hot day. Mickey's runners pounded the gravel track circuiting the golf course. He dodged electric carts and puddles from the previous night's heavy thunderstorm, greeting golfers, many of whom he knew, with nods in passing. He wasn't in the mood to chat. If they'd seen or heard about the leaked wedding photos, he didn't want to know about it.

He did keep an eye out for a pretty blonde attached by a leash to a tiny white dog. At the eighteenth hole he retraced his steps to the parking lot and then ran across the lawn past the tennis courts to the shoreline. Perhaps this morning Rachel hadn't walked Mopette farther than necessary to do its business in private. She must be exhausted. He allowed himself a self-congratulatory grin.

When he reached the sloping slab of pink granite overlooking the empty beach and sparkling lake, he stopped to catch his breath and take in the spectacular view that reminded him of Wisconsin's lake country. Two kayakers in bright orange life vests slid fast and low in parallel, their paddles briefly ruffling the glassy surface. The drone of a boat engine, as annoying as a mosquito's whine, disturbed the peace.

He pulled his water bottle from his waist pack and approached the line of white wood chairs at the infamous scenic outlook. The Rockery, the hotel called it.

On the nearest chair he recognized the purple and white flowers of one of Candy's bridesmaids' bouquets. A soggy folded note was tucked between wet, drooping roses. He extracted it. "Please return this to the front desk, attention Rachel," he read. Her missing bouquet.

He chugged some water, replaced the bottle, and gingerly lifted the bedraggled arrangement by stems wrapped in dirty, dangling ribbons that appeared to have been chewed by some animal.

A silver smartphone dropped out of the arrangement and smacked hard concrete. He picked it up. A spidery crack marred the screen. Worried he'd broken Rachel's cell, or that it had been damaged by the previous night's heavy rain, he pressed the power button. The screen brightened to reveal it was in camera mode. No password required. He tut-tutted.

She'd been taking pictures.

He held the unit in his hand. The full-face shot of Halden that currently flashed around the world had to have been snapped from the bridesmaids' side of the gazebo. Asta he discounted immediately. Tiffany'd been too busy sneaking a drink from bottles hidden in her bouquet.

That left Rachel.

Rachel, the aspiring cinematographer, who needed several thousand dollars for film school.

Terrible dread twisted his gut. He didn't want to believe it of the girl for whom he'd fallen like a ton of gold bricks. He accessed the phone's gallery folder and clicked on the most recent photo.

On Rachel's cracked screen, Halden's tearful face appeared. The exact wedding photo shared to millions of screens that morning. His ensuing agonized string of curses startled crows in the pines. Cawing, they took flight.

Through the red haze of fury clouding his brain, he tried to convince himself that she'd downloaded it from the Internet. But facts were facts. The bouquet with the concealed phone had obviously lain out in the rain all night. He unwillingly recalled that Rachel had had sufficient opportunity between the ceremony and the photo-shoot to upload and send photos to the media.

Despite the damning evidence, surely Candy's sweet cousin would never betray the bridal couple's privacy for money. Rachel was family! He'd return the smartphone and demand an explanation.

Chapter 19

How to Lose a Guy in Two Days

Breathing harshly, Mickey slammed the bedraggled bouquet onto the hotel Reception marble counter. To the busty front desk agent, he barked, "I'm looking for Rachel Lehmann. Give me her room number."

Juanita raised thin brows at his brusque demand. "She's working."

Mickey straightened. "Working?" Confusion stirred the dread icing his blood. "I'm looking for Rachel Lehmann, a bridesmaid in the wedding yesterday."

"I know who she is." Juanita smirked. "You'll find her on the third floor. Is that the bouquet she lost?"

"What's her room number?"

"The door will be open, sir," she answered cryptically, again with that satisfied twist to her lips.

Mickey snatched up the flowers and jogged to the stairwell.

To his right on the third floor, the west wing corridor was empty. To his left he spied a housekeeping cart. He approached the open door beside it. In the room a willowy blond chambermaid with black-framed glasses stripped sheets off the king bed.

The woman twisted to look at him. It was Rachel in ugly glasses and a baggy uniform. She froze. The color drained from her face.

"Mickey!"

"What the *hell* are you doing?" he shouted.

"Mickey, please. You'll wake the guests. Come in and close the door."

"*I'm* a guest. And apparently you're a *maid*."

Yet, he did as she requested for the sake of privacy. Inside the room he turned, pressed one hand against the closed door and bent his head, his back to her, heaving deep breaths in a vain attempt to bring wild emotions under control. The last thing on earth he expected to encounter was Rachel cleaning a room. What other lies had she told?

"Are you Candy's cousin?"

"No. Mickey—"

Holy Trickery. He made the logical deduction. Paps had their uses for publicity purposes, but stalking and infiltrating a private event in disguise was a despicable invasion of privacy. "You're paparazzo." He swiveled and spat the label like a swear word.

"*No*, Mick. I'm not." Her thin frame trembled. She sank onto the bed as if her legs no longer had the strength to support her.

Part of him wanted to believe her, regardless of the evidence in his pocket. He pulled out her phone, activated the screen, and thrust it close to her myopic eyes. "Did you take this photo of Halden?"

Rachel glanced at it. "Yes, but—"

He backed away, horrified, shattered. "That's all I need to know."

She'd betrayed him and his friends. Hot tears stung his eyes. He squeezed the lids tight. Given his track record with deceitful women, he of all men should've seen through Rachel's lies. He'd imagined himself in *love* with this unscrupulous fortune hunter. He felt like a fool.

In disgust he tossed the sad bouquet and her smartphone onto the dirty linens bundled on the floor. "Good-bye, Rachel," he choked.

Destroyed, he yanked open the door and marched down the hall, grief throttling his throat, searing pain slicing and dicing his heart.

She ran after him. "Mickey, let me explain."

He ignored her pathetic begging. *Oh no*, he'd never give her the opportunity to trick *him* again. The pain ignited fury. "Stay away from me," he raged, heedless of guests behind closed doors lining the hall. "Over my dead body you'll ever work in Hollywood."

★★★★★

Rachel impotently watched Mickey slam open the exit door to the stairwell and disappear out of her life.

Bitter tears coursed down her cheeks. She *did* take the photos with the intent to sell them. She *was* merely a hotel chambermaid. She *had* lied about being Candy's cousin.

Mickey deserved better.

Hope and heart crushed, shoulders drooping, Rachel returned to her duties.

★★★★★

When Halden turned on the water and the shower door slammed in the en suite bathroom, Candy pushed Mopette off her lap and rolled across the expanse of the bed to snag her smartphone from the night table. Eagerly she tapped on a new text message from Raynald. They'd agreed to limit exchanges in writing or by phone. Hackers exposed much that celebrities preferred to keep private.

Raynald's message contained only a number: *65*. Sixty-five thousand dollars! Deducting Raynald's 15 percent commission left her with $55,000. Enough to get the bank off her back and save her business.

[♫ "We're in the Money"]

Gleeful, she congratulated herself on reaping the profits from her own wedding photos, outsmarting the paparazzi for a change. Raynald negotiated the transaction through an "anonymous source," impossible to trace back to him.

Or more importantly, to her.

Candy eyed the television remote. She longed to view the wedding photos circling the globe.

No, too dangerous. If Halden walked in and noticed their wedding pics on the morning shows, he'd be livid. Her moral husband would erupt like that ancient volcano she'd learned about when researching Greek mythology before "running into" Halden the first time.

Her mouth dried. She'd relied on expert lovemaking skills on many occasions to calm down and distract a lover, but in this instance she feared sex wasn't the solution, at least not until Halden's initial reaction to the leaked photos blew over. Fortunately he planned to play a round of golf in a few minutes. That'd keep him occupied and away from screens for a couple of hours.

For extra insurance, she grabbed Halden's smartphone and shoved it between the mattress and box spring, then rolled to the middle of the bed. She assumed a seductive pose, artfully arranging the top sheet around her waist, leaving her breasts bare.

At the end of the bed, Mopette pounced on her toes under the covers.

"Mopette, come here." Candy patted the mattress at her side. When the pet obeyed, she buried her fingers in soft fur and lifted the dog high.

"My precious," she cooed, waggling Mopette in the air. "We're going to live in a stunning California beach house with a pool. I'll take you for a walk on the beach every day. Would you like that?"

Mopette yipped happily, loving the attention.

"That's right! No more slushy, cold New York winters."

The gargantuan diamond on Candy's left hand sparkled in rays streaming through the window. Relief displaced anxiety that had stalked her for weeks. Kudos to Raynald. His brain wave to sell his photos on her behalf meant she hadn't been forced to hock the diamond and replace it with a fake.

She lowered Mopette to the bed. "Lie down, my darling."

One hand absently scratching Mopette's ears, Candy extended her left arm to admire the two rings on her third finger. *Mrs. Halden Armstrong.* Happiness surged.

The previous summer, when her despicable sister lured Sir Timothy into her arms and between the sheets, Gwendy actually did her a favor. Instead of a mere knight, Candy married a prince. A Hollywood prince, that is. She chuckled softly. Next winter while Candy sat front and center at the televised *Golden Globe Awards* and *Academy Awards*, Gwendy would be enduring boring business dinners and stuffy fundraisers in Europe. *Good riddance!*

Triumphant, Candy pushed Mopette off the bed, relaxed into a seductive pose on fluffy down pillows, and waited for Halden.

Chapter 20

9 ½ Weeks Later

[♫ "Wish You Were Here"]

Marie-Eve expertly blended silvery-gray and fuchsia eye shadows on Rachel's closed right eyelid with the tip of a soft brush.

"The colors must look natural in artificial lights. Television high-definition cameras see every pore. Studio lighting is extremely hot and you sweat, *naturellement*, but it must not streak the makeup. The skin must breathe and also be flawless. *C'est difficile*," she murmured as she worked.

"It's difficult." Rachel corrected her friend automatically. Makeup was difficult. *Life without Mickey* was difficult. She pulled cotton bathrobe lapels protectively over her broken heart. It made no sense to dwell on what might have been. *Suck it up and move on.*

Marie-Eve shared her passion for show business, aspiring to be a professional makeup artist to the stars. They'd become close friends, making plans over meals in the Muskoka hotel staff dining room to relocate to Toronto, a Canadian hub of live theater and studios where films, network television shows, and cable series were shot.

At the end of the summer tourist season, the two women successfully applied for transfers to the luxury Sterling Inn Toronto overlooking Lake Ontario.

"I study the techniques for makeup as hard as you study for the show," Marie-Eve murmured as she carefully blended colors on the left eyelid.

"Preparation and opportunity lead to success."

"*Vraiment*, today is your big opportunity."

Winning the Kane-Armstrong love song challenge had opened Rachel's eyes to the possibility of making money with her photographic memory, that it was useful for more than acing tests in school. While watching a rerun of the long-running quiz show *Jeopardy!* a week after Mickey fled like she'd infect him with Ebola, Rachel had a lightbulb moment. Her knowledge of movie trivia surpassed that of a hundred wedding guests in the business. Surely she had a shot at winning a game or two on the new entertainment-focused Canadian spin-off, *EJ! Canada*?

In early August Rachel aced the qualifying fifty-question test for contestants. A producer called her to participate in two mock games, which she won easily. In fact, the impressed producer booked her for the inaugural mid-September taping. After weeks of memorizing entertainment industry facts in her spare time, the big day had finally arrived. Cross her fingers, she'd win a real game that afternoon.

Rachel heard Marie-Eve scrabbling through the contents of her enormous makeup kit on the hardwood floor of their tiny studio apartment. "May I open my eyes?"

"I search for the exact color of mascara. *Un moment*."

Rachel opened her eyes anyway. Through her new contact lenses she stared with astonishment at her reflection in the mirror above the vanity. Marie-Eve had worked artistic magic with air-brushed foundation, contouring, blush, and eye makeup. Rachel barely recognized herself.

"You made me look *better* than at the wedding."

"You have color from the sun, Rachel. You can now wear that shade of rose." She tilted her dark head in the direction of the deep pink wool suit jacket and matching fitted princess-cut dress with flared skirt hanging on the closet door.

The previous weekend the Québécoise fashionista had steered Rachel to Nordstrom in downtown Toronto. The clerk had folded Marie-Eve's expensive choices in tissue paper and boxed up stylish black stiletto heels. In addition, Rachel purchased the high-end makeup products that Marie-Eve recommended. The contents of the love song challenge gift card and Candy's generous $500 gratuity for replacing the missing bridesmaid disappeared into the cash register.

Marie-Eve had insisted that Rachel buy a second outfit, a seafoam-green tube with narrow straps that clung to Rachel's slim silhouette like it was sprayed on. Yet she sighed. Every dollar spent on her appearance cut into tuition savings for the University of Toronto's Cinema Studies Bachelor of Arts degree program. She'd abandoned her goal to become a cinematographer in favor of leveraging her encyclopedic knowledge of film.

"Are you certain buying *two* dresses was absolutely necessary? If I win today and make it to the next episode of *EJ! Canada*, I could've simply removed the pink jacket and added a scarf. *Voilà*—new outfit. Behind that high console no one can see my legs, let alone shoes that cost a small fortune."

Marie-Eve rolled her large, expressive brown eyes. "Must I repeat that television is about *entertainment*? Yes, your mind is *formidable*. But the audience prefers to watch a *belle* win the game rather than a geeky film historian in shapeless clothes and glasses, hmmm? Style gives you a *je ne sais quoi.*" She waved the mascara wand dramatically. "The women want to *be* you and the men want to f—"

"I get the picture," Rachel said dryly. "Appearance has entertainment value." She thought about the image she wanted to project. "Do you think that describing myself as a film critic for the taping sounds better? I'm not a graduate film historian."

Marie-Eve huffed. "Enough already with how you call yourself. You have more information about cinema inside that head than a dozen cinephiles."

"Film historian, then." Rachel swiveled her head left and right to admire fresh blond highlights in shoulder-length straight hair. "Pretending to be beautiful gives me confidence. *Merci*, Marie-Eve."

"What's with pretending? You *are* beautiful." She pointed the mascara wand at Rachel's reflection. "When will you believe that this image is your potential made visible? The makeup artist's role is to manifest its expression."

She chuckled as a thought occurred. "The other contestants, they will underestimate a beautiful woman. You will, how you say, wipe the floor with them. Now remain tranquil. I apply this mascara."

After Marie-Eve replaced the mascara in her kit, Rachel checked the time on her cracked smartphone screen. In ninety minutes they expected her in the television studio for a brief rehearsal, followed by taping of two shows that afternoon and into the evening if necessary.

Behind them, lingerie buried two comfy armchairs that flipped out into single beds. Marie-Eve had piled both her and Rachel's collections on the chairs in the hunt for the perfect set of bra, panties, and thigh-high sheer hose to wear under the outfits. Marie-Eve insisted that pretty undergarments gave one confidence. Rachel needed all the confidence she could muster.

Marie-Eve stepped back to assess her work, her lips pursed. She circled to view Rachel from every angle. "*Bon*, you are ready."

Rachel stood and hugged her friend. "Thank you *so* much. You're my fairy godmother."

Marie-Eve pursed her lips in denial. "You have good bones, *ma chère*. How you think Kim Kardashian looks when she quits her bed in the morning?"

Rachel laughed. She twirled across the floor on tiptoes, the cotton bathrobe flaring. If only Mickey could see her now.

Despite what she'd told Marie-Eve, today wasn't simply about winning money for tuition. Of course she aimed to win. But the road to redemption, and potentially to a relationship with a man as wonderful as Mickey someday, required that she step out of the shadows and strive to be her best self.

★★★★★

"You're divorcing Candy?" Mickey's jaw dropped. He quickly snapped it closed. Many Hollywood marriages imploded after the honeymoon period. However, two and a half months between a wedding and a separation set a new record in Mickey's circle of friends and associates.

Halden burned off leashed energy by striding the length of the living room in the luxury hotel suite he'd booked during the Toronto International Film Festival. "After I file the papers next week, it becomes a matter of public record. Until then, I'd appreciate it if you'd keep the news to yourself."

"Sure." Mickey sipped from the chilled bottle of Italian sparkling water Wendy handed him. She returned to her seat at the other end of the plush sofa they shared and picked up her smartphone to scroll through incoming texts. Obviously the announcement came as no surprise to her.

He eyed Wendy speculatively. Candy had fired her in front of everyone after the bouquet toss, so what was she doing here? *An affair with Halden? Nah.* He dismissed the idea. Halden's set jaw and scowl projected anger. The only chemistry in the room was the explosive kind. Strong emotion seethed under Halden's normally easygoing countenance.

"I wanted to tell you privately," Halden continued. "You being my groomsman and all. We've both been crazy busy since the wedding, you with your agency start up, me in preproduction for *Apollo: Intergalactic War*. When I heard you were in Toronto for the film festival, I asked Wendy to arrange our meet."

Curiosity had Mickey leaning forward, forearms on thighs. A dozen possible explanations crowded his brain, but aloud he merely inquired, "You okay? Anything I can do?"

Halden stopped pacing and planted himself in front of Mickey, arms crossed, legs wide in his familiar Apollo stance, although this was no act. "Candy sold the wedding photos."

Mickey's heart turned over. "The photos leaked to the media the day after the wedding?"

"The very same." Halden's glacial stare represented the tip of the iceberg of the depths of his outrage.

Guilt clawed Mickey's gut. Easygoing Halden had few enemies, but that didn't make him a pushover. Despite her greed and betrayal, a young chambermaid was no match for a man of Halden's power and influence. A protective instinct had constrained Mickey from telling Halden the truth these many weeks since the wedding: Rachel sold those photos.

Upon returning to LA, he frequently woke with wet cheeks from dreams that left him suffused with a primal sense of loss. Setting aside his private pain, he steeled himself to set the record straight in order to save his friend's marriage.

"You have it all wrong. Remember Rachel, Candy's cousin?"

"Rachel was another of Candy's pawns." Bitterness laced Halden's voice. "She wasn't actually Candy's cousin."

"*You* knew that?" Now he was surprised.

"Sure. Candy obviously had to explain, at least to me and her parents, how a 'cousin,'" he pantomimed air quotes, "manifested out of nowhere when her maid of honor failed to show. The chambermaid fit the bridesmaid's dress. I agreed to keep her hotel employee status secret for the sake of appearances."

For half a minute Mickey digested the fact that Halden had been aware all along that Rachel was a maid. So Rachel and Candy were in cahoots. Was Rachel working as an undercover paparazzo for Candy? Pain squeezed his heart. He had to know.

"If Candy sold the photos, where did she get them?"

"I have proof that the skinny photographer friend of Candy's took them."

Mickey belatedly recalled Halden's annoyance when the photographer hopped about the gazebo during the ceremony. "Raynald?"

"That's the guy. He sold them on behalf of Candy."

Mickey wiped a hand down the side of his face and slumped against the back of the sofa. Things didn't compute. He'd seen the incriminating photos on Rachel's cell with his own eyes.

"I became suspicious when Candy faked being upset by the exploitation of our private moments. She's no actor." Halden began to stride back and forth across the carpet again. "Mick, it's like a love spell wears off, and the beautiful princess is revealed to be an ugly witch."

Mickey nodded, recognizing the film reference. "*The Quest for the Golden Necklace.*"

Halden abruptly halted and swiveled on one leather-booted foot to look him in the eye. "You negotiated my first speaking role as a knight in that film. With it I obtained my ACTRA card and entry into the business. You had my back."

"Always." Emboldened by Halden's expressed gratitude for the small part he played in his rise to stardom, Mickey crossed his fingers that what he was about to say wouldn't destroy their friendship. "Hal, I never told you I discovered wedding pictures on Rachel's phone."

Halden's brows lifted halfway to thick blond hair. "What? You believe *Rachel* sold her photos? You're wrong." He pulled up a chair to sit and face Mickey on the sofa. "After I returned to LA, without telling Candy, I immediately hired a private investigator to trace the leak. I provided a list of the wedding guests and hotel service staff, including Rachel. He traced a sixty-five thousand dollar payment from a photo agency to Raynald's bank account. I put two and two together and figured out their game plan. When I confronted Candy, she burst into tears and confessed."

"Holy Heartbreak, Halden!" he commiserated.

Logically, a millionaire's bride didn't need money *that* badly, but, then again, many Hollywood celebrities pursued media attention at any cost. Deep inside, a tsunami of relief and joy washed away cruel disappointment, leaving shame in its wake. Mickey leaped to his feet. He had to find Rachel and apologize! He'd disastrously misjudged the quirky, talented girl.

But Halden wasn't finished unburdening himself. It was Mickey's turn to pace with leashed energy while Halden continued. "The next day I moved Candy and that toy dog of hers into the Beverley Hills Hotel. I changed the locks on the beach house. She's begging me to agree to marriage counseling. Forget it. Candy betrayed my trust. She exploited our wedding for personal profit. I'll *never* forgive her." Massive shoulders quaked with indignation. Nordic-blue eyes misted.

Wendy sprang from the sofa to lay a small comforting hand on Halden's muscular shoulder. Mickey paused beside the pair, brows lifted. Halden caught the unspoken query, and his features relaxed for the first time that afternoon. His famous grin slashed his handsome face.

"You dog. It's not what you think. Candy fired Wendy in Muskoka. After I kicked Candy out of the beach house, I hired Wendy to become *my* personal assistant."

She didn't waste any time, Mickey thought without rancor. Lovestruck, star struck, whatever label you wanted to apply, Wendy in her low-cut tight sweater had it bad for Halden. Maybe as bad as Mickey had it for Rachel.

"I have to talk to Rachel. I'll rent a car and drive up to Muskoka."

"Hold on," Wendy counseled. She waggled the phone in her free hand. "Rachel isn't responding to my messages so I texted the Sterling Inn Muskoka's general manager and received a response in less than a minute. Throwing Halden's name around has its perks." A satisfied smile illuminated her clever face. "I have an update on her coordinates. Rachel transferred to the Sterling Inn Toronto after the summer season. Her current manager texted me a few seconds ago that Rachel booked the day off to be a contestant on an entertainment-themed Canadian spin-off of *Jeopardy!* called *EJ! Canada*."

She laughed at the men's astounded expressions. "Rachel won the movie love song challenge at your wedding day brunch, Halden. She has a unique talent for trivia."

"Don't I know it." Mickey pulled out his smartphone and launched the GPS application. "You're the *best*, Wendy. Where's the show being taped?"

Wendy tapped the name of a television studio into a map app. "The taping is at this address." She held her screen so Mickey could type it into his app.

Halden wrapped a long arm around Wendy's waist and pulled her in for a brief hug. "Wendy, you're awesomely efficient."

The curvy, petite woman stilled, but Mickey noted the joy radiating from every fiber of her being. The PA adored Halden. He fervently hoped, for the sake of Halden's future happiness, that he fell in love with the true treasure at his side rather than in lust with another beautiful gold digger.

However, his own love life took priority right now. Would Rachel forgive him for doubting her integrity? Mickey leaned over to kiss Wendy's cheek. He pumped Halden's hand.

"Mickey needs a ride," the ultra-competent assistant gently suggested.

"Take my limo," Halden invited.

Wendy nodded and busily tapped her cell screen. In seconds a ding announced a response. "The driver will be waiting at the front entrance."

Mickey thanked them both profusely. Wendy accompanied him in order to unlock the suite door. "There's a florist in the hotel lobby," she hinted. "Rachel is one of a kind. I like her a lot."

With the formidable PA's seal of approval ringing in his ears, Mickey bolted down the hall to the elevator.

Chapter 21

She's All That

Thirty minutes of excruciating stop-and-go rush-hour traffic later, Mickey impatiently stepped onto the sidewalk in front of the television studio, a dozen red roses clutched in a fist, and dismissed Halden's rented limo and driver.

Flashing his talent agent credentials convinced a security guard to let Mickey slip in to the small *EJ! Canada* studio during a break in the taping. In vain he scanned the audience for an empty seat. The burly bald guard motioned him to stand to his right against the rear wall beside the exit.

Down on the set under bright metal halide lights, in the returning champion position behind the console, stood Rachel, stunning in a hot green dress that molded to her figure. The director gave the signal to roll tape.

The game show host, a younger clone of Alex Trebek, the Canada-born longtime host of *Jeopardy!*, read out the next answer. "This Canadian actor starred in *Speed* with Sandra Bullock." The attentive audience remained quiet as it waited for a contestant to respond in the form of a question.

Rachel clicked the handheld signal device in an imperceptible lightning movement. "Who is Keanu Reeves," she said, not a hint of a question in her confident tone.

"Correct," responded the host.

"*Hollywood or Bus* for three hundred," Rachel requested.

Few squares remained under the six categories on the massive game board behind the host, indicating the double round to be in the final stages. Mickey noted the dollar values on the board were half those of the flagship US version of *Jeopardy!* He speculated that the Canadian producers didn't have equivalent access to US network and syndication revenue. California had a larger population than the entire country of Canada.

Concentrating on the questions, Rachel appeared oblivious to the cameras, the two grim male contestants to her left, and the audience applauding every correct answer. One by one, Rachel knocked off the remaining squares, adding hundreds to her runaway lead.

During the break between the double round and final question, Mickey shifted his focus from Rachel to compare the contestants' scores and anticipate the bets. Rachel ranked first, with $9,900. The scores of the two male contestants were $1,300 and $2,800 respectively. Would Rachel minimize her bet to walk away with almost ten grand in case she answered incorrectly, or would she risk it all in a bold attempt to maximize her winnings?

He thought back to their time together. At the gazebo before the wedding rehearsal, Rachel hung back, shy and lacking confidence. But he held no illusions that it was *he* who seduced *her* after the wedding reception. When she wanted something, she went for it.

The final question flashed on an overhead monitor visible to the audience. "Three sci-fi television series—*The*

X-Files, *Stargate SG-1*, and *Battlestar Galactica*—have this in common," intoned the handsome host.

The studio audience hushed for thirty suspenseful seconds as Merv Griffin's "Think!" tune played over the speakers. The three contestants scribbled on their pads.

Then it was time for the first reveal. The male contestant farthest from Rachel shook his head and frowned as his answer, "Who is producer?" was declared incorrect. His bet of $650 was deducted and the total on his scoreboard dropped to $650.

The middle contestant answered "What are filmed in Vancouver?"

"Correct," the host said, accompanied by a smattering of applause. The contestant's all-or-nothing bid of $2,799 increased his score to $5,599.

If Rachel had similarly made an all-or-nothing bet to maximize her winnings, and answered incorrectly, she'd lose the game. Mickey held his breath along with the audience.

Rachel's neat handwriting appeared. "What are all filmed in Vancouver, British Columbia?"

"Correct," the host enthused. Tumultuous applause erupted at the reveal of Rachel's strategic $4,299 bet. Right or wrong, she'd cleverly guaranteed the returning championship and the opportunity to win a third game. Her daily score ratcheted up to $14,199.

The host listened through his earpiece and then announced, smiling broadly, "That brings Rachel to a two-day total of $22,599!"

Every person in the audience rose to give her a standing ovation. "Rachel, Rachel, Rachel," they chanted.

Under cover of the hoots and whistles, the security guard at Mickey's side commented out of the corner of his mouth, "That babe dominated both episodes from the start of the clock. I've watched *Jeopardy!* for years, am a huge fan. Jeez Louise, she's a phenomenon. Never seen a contestant as quick to hit that button as her. You her agent?"

Mickey never took his eyes off Rachel, who appeared stunned at the audience's reaction. "I'm her man." *More accurately, I hope to be, if she'll forgive me.*

The security guard glanced down at the bouquet Mickey held tucked in the crook of one arm. "Shoulda guessed. Tell her to apply to *Jeopardy!* in California," he advised. "That's the place to win big bucks."

"Oh, I agree she belongs in California." *With me.*

Down on the set, Rachel shaded her eyes from the bright overhead lights, peered up into the darkened audience seating, and waved to acknowledge the applause. Impulsively Mickey made a move toward the center stairs down to the set.

The security guard slammed a hand on his shoulder. "Hold on, buddy. The camera's rolling live-to-tape, with simultaneous editing. You don't want her standing ovation to be edited out, do you?"

"No, sir." With difficulty he controlled impatience. This was Rachel's moment.

Rachel and the two men left their positions behind the console. Rachel teetered on ridiculously high heels in a short green dress that showcased her amazing long legs. Mickey held his breath until she safely reached the handsome host and swiveled to face the camera. It zoomed in and filled the studio monitors with a close-up of her sweet but sexy smile, teary eyes, and regular features enhanced by expertly applied makeup. His heart filled with pride. The audience adored the package—a whip-smart beauty who took calculated risks.

In Toronto that afternoon, three thousand miles from Tinseltown on the other side of the continent, Rachel's star began its ascent.

With brave smiles, the other contestants approached to shake Rachel's hand, an obvious ploy to grab screen time in the wrap-up. The host slid an arm possessively around her trim waist and invited the television audience to watch the next episode to find out if Rachel's winning streak continued.

At the prospect of several episodes as returning champion, Mickey switched into agent mode. After the shows aired, he'd have no difficulty arranging interviews on *ET Canada*, Canadian morning shows, and possibly a guest spot on a low-rated US late-night talk show.

Then reality intruded. He'd been such an ass. Why should Rachel even agree to speak to him, let alone sign as his client? He decided to hook Rachel up with a respected agent and provide behind-the-scenes assistance to launch her career, even if she refused to have anything to do with him personally.

He owed her that much.

The director signaled "cut" and the end of the segment. A petite dark-haired woman in torn jeans and a T-shirt sprinted onto the set and enveloped Rachel in a big hug, almost knocking her off her feet. Rachel stepped out of the treacherous heels and hugged her back. They laughed and jumped up and down with excitement.

Preserving the flowers from being crushed by holding them high above his head, Mickey pushed his way through the people surging up the stairs to the exit and descended to the set. He approached the women from behind.

At his tap on her shoulder, Rachel swung around, gasped, turned pale, then flushed pink. "Mickey!"

He thrust the red roses wrapped in cellophane at her. "Congratulations, Rachel." His throat trapped some vowels, and he cleared it before adding, "You were *awesome.*"

"Oh my gods." Rachel latched onto the other woman's arm to support herself. "Mickey, what are *you* doing here?"

In close, he forgot to breathe, lost in absorbing Rachel's essence—her startled gold-flecked brown eyes, faint floral perfume, expressive features, and a willowy body he longed to hug. His mind blanked. He fastened his gaze on Rachel's lush rosebud lips, so close, so… On this occasion, one of very few times in his life, Mickey was speechless.

Instead of accepting the flowers, Rachel maneuvered her friend forward. "This is my roommate, Marie-Eve Tremblay. She did my makeup today and for…for the Kane-Armstrong wedding."

"Very nice to meet you," he said to Marie-Eve. With vision still adjusting to strong overhead lighting, he squinted at the attractive woman. "You look familiar."

"I styled your hair for the wedding." Marie-Eve's sexy French accent relayed chagrin.

"Ahhh." He flashed her an apologetic smile. Men rarely noticed staff. If Rachel hadn't been a bridesmaid or a wedding guest, he probably wouldn't have noticed her either. He shuffled from foot to foot, feeling shallower than a puddle.

The women stared at him expectantly—Marie-Eve with arms defensively crossed and mouth in a disapproving pout, Rachel's dark eyes round and unreadable.

He cleared his throat again. "I apologize." He bowed to Marie-Eve. "I apologize on behalf of myself and all ignorant men who sit in your salon chair without appreciating your beauty and skills."

Marie-Eve rolled her eyes. "He's a charmer, this one," she said to Rachel. "No wonder you fell in love."

"Marie-Eve!"

Taking Rachel's mortified expression and lack of denial as promising signs, and mindful of the microphone boom hanging above their heads, Mickey stepped in to whisper, "I apologize for taking off before hearing you out." He extended the bouquet, and this time Rachel gathered the roses to her chest.

"Mickey," she breathed, dropping her nose deep into the flowers to inhale. Her shoulders relaxed.

He assumed he was out of the doghouse and back into her good graces. *Whew.*

Then her chin lifted. Intelligent eyes slitted with suspicion. "Is it a coincidence that an *agent* shows up on the exact day of my *EJ! Canada* taping, weeks after you dumped me?" The accusation slid off her tongue as smooth and cool as ice cubes.

He held up both hands and backed off a step in feigned shock. Anxious to disavow the implication he wanted to capitalize on Rachel's success in the same way he'd tried to sign Tiffany for a cut of her potential Bond-girl gig revenue, he sputtered, "I'm in town for the film festival and tracked you down. Or, to be honest, Wendy did it for me. The fact that you're a contestant on *EJ! Canada* is a wonderful surprise."

"Oh yeah?" She remained skeptical.

Yeah, she'd had plenty of time to analyze his character after he bolted without giving her a chance to explain the photos on her smartphone. His attempt to sign Tiffany illustrated how dealmakers often resorted to manipulation to get signatures on contracts and money in their pockets. The only thing separating him from those sharks without consciences was that at least he considered the potential impact of Tiffany York's drinking on her reputation, and didn't want any part of on-set problems that could destroy her career.

The lurking presence of the blatantly eavesdropping host intruded on his awareness. Mickey cupped each woman's elbow and propelled them to the edge of the set. "We'll talk, but this isn't the place. Will you permit me to take you both out for a celebratory dinner?"

"Sure." Rachel seized on the suggestion, no doubt wanting Marie-Eve's support for what she anticipated to be a difficult conversation.

Marie-Eve cut her off. "But no, Mr. McNichol, you are too polite. I make my excuses with thanks."

"Another evening then," Mickey insisted. "I'll be in town the rest of the week."

Marie-Eve glanced from Rachel's flushed face to his. "Of course. If you have the spare time for eating, Mickey." The roommate reached for the bouquet of red roses. "Rachel, I will put these flowers in water at our apartment. I expect not to see you until tomorrow at work." An elaborate, suggestive wink reinforced the implication in her words.

Grinning, Marie-Eve trotted off the set and left them to it.

★★★★★

Rachel led Mickey to a quiet corner booth in her favorite brew pub in Toronto's historic Distillery District. Hundred-year-old warehouses had been converted into restaurants, art galleries, and boutiques with exposed brick walls and retro industrial decor. At seven o'clock on a midweek evening, the dining area remained half empty. By nine, film festival revelers filled the place to capacity.

The server arrived to take their order. Rachel selected one of the local craft beers, and Mickey echoed her choice.

When the server departed, she waited for Mickey to speak, her mind spinning with possible reasons he'd sought her out after all these weeks. Perhaps the apology was intended to soften her up for another convenient hook-up. Maybe he wanted to put the brief, passionate relationship to bed, so to speak.

They faced each other across the wood table, a flickering candle in a glass jar between them. Mickey sported a black leather jacket, white dress shirt open at the neck, a fashionable couple of days' stubble darkening his jaw, and thick silver-threaded hair falling over his high forehead. He was sophisticated. Sexy. Adorable.

Out of my league.

"You look fantastic." Mickey's expression conveyed genuine appreciation.

"Better than on the last occasion we met," she recalled wryly, a hitch in her breath. "Mick, what's changed? Why are you here?"

Mickey reached across the table for her hand. Fingers tensely intertwined in her lap, she resisted the invitation.

He dumped me and broke my heart. Now he's back. Why?

He retracted the hand and drew it down one side of his unshaven face. "Rach, I can't find the words to tell you how sorry I am that I misjudged you."

Confusion rattled Rachel's stiff outward calm. "Misjudged me how? I *am* a chambermaid. I work at the Sterling Inn Toronto."

"I know. Wendy told me this afternoon."

"Candy's personal assistant?"

"Actually, Wendy recently became Halden's PA. They're in Toronto for the international film festival." He paused while the server placed frosted pints of beer on the table. After the server walked out of earshot, he continued.

"Halden revealed this afternoon that Candy sold their wedding photos to the media."

Rachel had guessed that no one but Raynald could possibly have snapped the Kane-Armstrong photos that trended on the Internet and television after the wedding. Other than the official photographer, and herself, of course, Raynald had been the only person at the center of the action with a camera in hand.

"Candy must have sold Raynald's photos."

Mickey paused in the act of sipping his beer and nodded.

"Even though Candy attacked Raynald with her bouquet?" She worked it out. "Makes sense she'd be terrified Raynald would sell his photos of Tiffany's collapse along with the other pics."

"Sixty-five thousand dollars is a good incentive to repair the friendship."

Sixty-five thousand! Rachel's media contact had only offered twenty grand. She bit her lip, awash in guilt, yet amazed the leaked photos were worth so much. "That's all very interesting, but what does it have to do with misjudging me?"

Pushing his beer glass aside, Mickey placed both forearms on the table, leaned in, and spoke low. "When I scrolled through the wedding photos on your phone, I figured *you* sold them to pay for film school tuition."

Heat flamed her skin. "I did no such thing."

Steel-gray eyes softened with sincerity in the light of the flickering candle. "I realize that now. I am very sorry. I'm such a jerk for jumping to the conclusion that you betrayed Halden."

Rachel's heart fluttered inside her ribs like a bird frantic to escape a cage. He had no clue she'd been a click of an email away from betraying Halden. Telling Mickey the truth meant watching disgust curl his fine mouth, meant watching him bolt out of her life again, this time forever. Every cell in her body begged that he retain a good opinion of her.

But if I hide the truth in order to keep him, I'll be living a lie.

Filling her lungs with calming energy, as practiced for that day's television taping, she chose the path that would let her sleep at night. She squeezed eyelids closed, not brave enough to watch angry rejection twist his features yet again.

"Mick, I did need money for my education. I—I hid my phone in my bouquet and snapped dozens of pictures during the wedding. I almost sold them. I had a buyer lined up." A tear slid down a cheek burning with shame. "I'm a terrible person."

Mickey remained uncharacteristically silent. She opened her eyes, fearing the worst. Mickey leaned away from the table, away from her, his expression unfathomable in dim light. "You didn't sell them, Rach. That's what counts." Gruff emotion in his tone projected comfort, not censure.

"Only because I discovered Halden puts so much value on his privacy. I couldn't hurt him, not for all the money in the world." Liquid pain brimmed, overflowed. She buried her face in her hands, shoulders shaking with silent sobs. "I'm so sorry for what I did, Mickey."

"*Almost* did, Rachel. That's the crux." She heard a chair scrape on the hardwood floor. In seconds he pulled her upright, gently pressed her head into the notch between his neck and shoulder, and crushed her to his muscular chest.

"The base desires for inappropriate sex, money, power, and fame lead people astray. Character brings them back in line." Soothing swipes of a palm played over her rigid back. Warm, steady breaths stirred hair near her ear. "I adore your character," he whispered. "In fact, I'm crazy in love with your character."

"Mick, I don't deserve you," she mumbled into his shirt collar.

A puff of air in her ear accompanied a dismissive snort. "Please don't put me on a pedestal, Rach. Exactly like you and everyone else in the world, I regularly struggle to do the right thing. Temptation is powerful." He threaded fingers through her hair. "I have a proposal for you."

"What is it?" Rachel lifted her head and stiffened, anxious he'd tarnish the sterling sentiments by asking to become her agent, or, the gods forbid, ask her to marry him. She wasn't ready…

One strong finger tipped her chin up, forcing tear-blurred eyes to meet his somber gaze. "We'll keep each other honest. Deal?"

Oh, Mickey. Love spilled out of the heart she'd sealed up tight. "Deal."

Chapter 22

Happy Together

Mickey slipped his key card into his room's lock in Toronto's iconic Royal York Hotel, held the door for Rachel, and flipped a light switch that activated a desk lamp.

Rachel hesitated, pulse galloping. The last time she'd entered Mickey's hotel room she'd been sure of what she wanted—him. Given her circumstances, she'd realistically desired one fabulous night together, a fling, nothing more. Months later, his return and apology meant one thing, and it scared the pants off her.

He's serious about me.

She entered and cast a trained eye over the upscale room, taking in tailored charcoal velvet curtains, pristine bedding, and designer furnishings. A champagne bottle cooled in a polished bucket on a stand beside the desk. A pool of light from the desk lamp illuminated a platter of chocolate-covered strawberries and delightful frosted *petits fours*.

She removed patent leather stilettos worth a week's paycheck, bounced on her toes over to the platter, and popped a tiny pink iced cake into her mouth. The confection disintegrated in a burst of cotton-candy sensation. *Heavenly.*

"I called ahead and asked for bite-sized cakes to be sent to the room. I remembered how much you enjoyed them at the rehearsal dinner." He shrugged out of his jacket and threw it over the back of a chair.

"So thoughtful." Her heart melted along with a mint frosted cake on her tongue. "A perfect ending to a perfect day."

He waggled his brows. "The day's not over yet. Champagne?"

She flung herself lengthwise across the bed, then thought better of it and hastily sat up. "Champagne would be great." *And might calm my nerves.*

Rachel scooted off the edge of the bed, switched on the bedside lamps, removed the decorative pillows, and turned down the bedspread.

"Hey," Mickey handed her a flute of bubbly, entwined fingers in hers, and tugged her over to the upholstered bench at the foot of the bed. "Sit beside me and relax. I didn't bring you here to entice you into having sex."

She raised one plucked brow to call him on that outrageous statement.

He chuckled. "Not right away, then. Let's talk."

"Didn't we cover everything over dinner?"

They'd chatted in the restaurant for two hours over gourmet burgers, sweet potato fries, and kale salad, until the rising noise level drove them out to the street and into a cab to Mickey's downtown hotel. They'd shared their histories, their favorite actors, and the movies that made them laugh or cry—casual conversation anyone might have with a friend. Yet the intense focus as he listened, the genuine interest in her opinions, how he seemed to read her mind and anticipate her thoughts—they combined to make it the most intimate, soul-baring two hours of her life.

He cleared his throat. "At the restaurant we never discussed how *you* feel about us."

She gulped. In her experience, men *never* wanted to discuss feelings. Show, not tell, was standard *modus operandi*.

Noticing her panicked expression, he offered, "I'll start."

She blew out the breath she'd been holding. A sinewy strong forearm slid around her waist and drew her tight. Through his thin shirt, she felt rapid heartbeats vibrate against her side. Mickey's smooth, confident demeanor masked nerves as wired as her own.

"We had a rocky start to a relationship. Instant attraction, at least on my side." He tilted his handsome dark head inquiringly. When she nodded agreement, he continued. "Followed by a huge misunderstanding. I want to start over. Are you game?"

"With all those starlets to choose from," she squeaked through a throat tight with mystified tension, "why me?"

"Because you're one of a kind, Rach. You make me laugh." When her face scrunched in embarrassment, he clarified, "In a good way, always." He lifted her hand and kissed moisturizer-softened skin. "I enjoy being with you. And not just in bed. I've never met any girl, in California, in Wisconsin, anywhere, with your spark and special talent."

Spark and special talent, eh?

Before her success on *EJ! Canada* that day, she'd have dismissed those compliments as ridiculous. Of all the people in her twenty-two years of life, only Mickey had ever noticed and valued her photographic memory and fascination for film trivia. Only Mickey had ever made her feel special. His genuine respect had opened her eyes to the potential of an entertainment industry career based on her unique talent, instead of a job behind a camera watching others shine. Bottom line, Mickey had been good for her.

He made me want to be a better person. Gods permitting, I'll be good for him, too.

Rachel shoved aside all the logical reasons why a long distance relationship with a Californian was unworkable, and listened to her heart. "I'm willing to start over, Mickey."

She rose and, mindful of the maid who had to clean the room the next day, placed their half-empty champagne flutes carefully on the nearest nightstand. Then she gripped his hands, pulled him to his feet, and curled fingers possessively around lean, muscled biceps. "Kiss me before I change my mind."

Swiftly Mickey lowered his mouth with pent-up passion. His tongue slid between her lips, thick, insistent. One hand unzipped the seafoam tube dress, exposing bare skin. A flick of an expert finger, and the bra unhooked. Fevered hands sought and cupped her breasts. Thumbs flicked exquisitely sensitive nipples.

Rachel broke the lip-lock, drew apart to busily unfasten his trouser button and zipper over a herculean bulge, and barely registered when the outrageously expensive dress slid down her body and crumpled on the carpet.

He slid an arm under her knees and lifted her onto the bed. "Don't move."

White shirttail hanging, trousers gathered about his ankles, he race-wobbled like a penguin to his suitcase on a stand, scrabbled with both hands through clothing, and finally extracted a box of condoms with a whoop.

Rachel giggled, thrilled by Mickey's enthusiasm, his joyful abandon. So much for that charming, sophisticated veneer he projected to the world. Maybe they had more wackiness in common than she thought.

While Mickey ditched his clothing, she rolled down and discarded her sheer hose, then flung her pink lace bra onto the lampshade, followed by the scrap of matching lace thong. She bounced off the bed and dashed across the carpet to press her bare tush against the closed bathroom door.

"Mickey, darling." He swiveled. Eyes goggled. Holding her arms out to him, she invited, "Shower?"

Mickey groaned and fumbled with the condom wrapper. "Don't think I'll make it into the shower, sweetheart." Seconds later his muscled chest flattened her against the door. His clad granite-hard rod nudged her folds, found them wet and ready. Yet he hesitated.

Rachel clutched his shoulders for support, tilted her pelvis. "What are you waiting for?"

"Standing? Are you sure?"

She fisted his bulging member and positioned it. "Oh Mick, I'd do you anywhere. Standing, sitting, even in the elevator."

He thrust once, filling her with sweet pleasure. "There are security cameras in elevators."

"Guess what? As of today I'm comfortable in front of the camera."

He braced one arm on the door behind her, slid his thick shaft slickly over all those lovely nerve endings deep inside. "You'll be featured on *EJ! Canada* when today's shows air in a few weeks. Can't risk leaked Internet exposure."

"You're no fun," she pretend-pouted. With each thrust, urgency built. Her knees turned to jelly. *His magic wand is driving me out of my mind.*

Between pants that tickled her ear, he muttered, "We'll wear disguises."

Despite the liquid fire tracing her nerves, she laughed.

"You're teasing me," he accused, his breathing hot and jagged and thunderous against her neck as he fought manfully to control his release.

"You...are...teasing...*me*," she managed to reply.

Mickey adjusted the angle of his shaft, homed in on her G-spot, and rubbed a thumb over her swollen, primed nub. Her mind blanked as shattering pulses of electric fire ricocheted from crotch to nipples to toes. She held on for dear life, fingertips digging into Mickey's back, as he slammed against her crotch once, twice, and then exploded inside her clenched canal.

"Holy Fireworks, Rachel," Mickey gasped when he could speak. He gently pressed his mouth to her damp neck, her cheek, her soft, swollen lips. "I'll never let you go again."

★★★★★

A sunbeam arrowed between the velvet curtains, waking Rachel. She rolled off Mickey's chest and onto her side of the soft bed. The empty champagne bottle rested upside down in a bucket on the floor nearby.

Mickey plumped up pillows, lowered into a reclining position, and tucked Rachel under one arm. "I could get used to this."

"Mmmmmm," Rachel murmured. She loved the way his chest vibrated under her cheek when he spoke. She stretched, and a fragile tendril of happiness unfurled from her heart.

"Move in with me."

Stunned, she levered on one elbow to assess his sincerity. "Move to LA? You're not serious."

He returned her gaze steadily. "I'm seriously in love. These weeks without you have been pure misery. I want to wake up beside you every morning and kiss you like this."

For several minutes Rachel surrendered to fervent kisses that made her heart sing and her loins ache with desire. She loved him with all her heart.

Finally she came up for air, flipped on her back, and propped herself on the pillows beside him, palms pancaked between breasts to calm a galloping heartbeat. "Give a girl a minute to think."

Mickey bent his dark head to lick the closest nipple. "No thinking necessary. Your *EJ! Canada* winnings today would pay for a year's tuition at a US state college, correct?"

"It would cover the foreign student premium," she qualified, squirming under the sensuous caresses. "The Canadian government does not tax lottery or game show prizes."

He switched to the other budded nipple, and she threw her head back. Her fingers curled in to clutch swaths of his thick hair. Spiraling arousal fogged her brain. "Mickey, please, I can't think."

"Think about this." His talented lips spread in a cocky grin. "I rent a guesthouse in Hollywood Hills, home of the American Film Institute. The California State University, Los Angeles, is a short commute from my place."

Oh my gods. Mickey opened the door to a future that fulfilled head *and* heart. Like thousands of girls with stars in their eyes before her, she squealed, "Hollywood, here I come!"

[♫ "Hollywood"]

Mickey watched her from under hooded eyelids. "Of course, you don't have to go to college. If you'd prefer to remain a chambermaid, there are plenty of Hollywood mansions and hotels in need of staff."

Rachel bounced onto her knees and thumped him with her pillow. "Not on my radar."

"I didn't think so," Mickey said smugly.

She sat back on her heels. "But now that you mention it, I'll need to earn enough to pay for the rest of my college expenses. I may win the next *EJ! Canada* episode, gods willing, but if not, is there any chance you can put me in touch with the producer of *Jeopardy!*?"

"I have contacts." He crossed his arms over his bare chest and quirked a brow. "What do I get in return?"

Rachel tossed the pillow on the floor and draped her naked body on top of his. "Me."

Read on for an excerpt of *Seduced by the Screenwriter*, Book 2.

Seduced by the SCREENWRITER

Description

Love scenes wearing movie costumes—a hot romance with a playlist.

Ex-cop Catrina Turner is lonely. After a traumatic recovery dive she quit the force and ran away to remote Muskoka with Titan, her retired police service dog. They provide winter security for luxury lake houses owned by rich celebrities. Her PTSD, a closely-held secret, makes a relationship impossible…until a handsome visitor makes a tempting proposal.

Screenwriter Chett de Groot needs a hit to save his career. He accepts a film star's offer to use her secluded lake house as a writing retreat, and discovers a closet full of her old movie costumes.

Bored, freezing in Muskoka and desperate for inspiration, Chett entices the beautiful security guard to wear costumes and role-play in seduction scenes. They discover how *satisfying* acting can be. Soon Catrina is ad-libbing passionate lines in scorching "performances" that knock Chett's thermal socks off.

A film producer makes Chett an offer that will put him back in the game. But if Catrina finds out what Chett did to close the deal, will he lose her forever?

Excerpt: Chapter 1

Baby, It's Cold Outside

A knee-deep layer of fresh snow blocked the long laneway to the five-thousand-square-foot summer home owned by Catrina's most important client, Jenna Jordan, Hollywood movie star.

"It's our lucky day! The plow hasn't been by yet. I'll need the snowshoes, Titan," Catrina informed her German shepherd, who wagged his tail at the thrum of pleasure in her voice. She reached into the cargo area of her beat-up SUV to fish out new aluminum frames.

The awkward foot extensions firmly attached, her down parka zipped, Catrina adopted a wide stance and swung her legs forward, each step a delight as the snowshoe sank a couple of inches into powder. Titan bounded ahead to sniff rabbit and deer tracks. Pine and spruce branches sagged with sparkling snow.

The crisp, sunny early January day in pristine forest, the opportunity to fill her lungs with pure air—it all validated the decision to quit her job as a Toronto Police constable in order to provide security services to millionaire owners of exclusive waterfront properties on Lake Muskoka—Canada's summer playground for the fabulously rich and famous.

No boss. No shifts. No traffic!

Her fledgling stress-free business amounted to a paid vacation year round. So far she had security contracts with ten wealthy waterfront home owners and enough income to pay the bills. Her big break came the previous summer when Jenna signed on as a client after firing the security guard who'd helped himself to several bottles in the wine cellar and let mice roam the interior.

A whiff of wood smoke stopped her short. Jenna's residence was supposed to be vacant. The Hollywood actor never visited between September and June. Now on high alert, Catrina punched rapidly through the snow another quarter mile to a curve that provided a sight line to the main house.

A tendril of smoke indeed curled from the chimney. A faint, rhythmic *thwack*, *thwack* disrupted the tranquility of the isolated property. She sucked frigid air deep into a tight chest. Titan, sensing the tension in his mistress, growled deep in his throat.

"Shhh," she commanded. "Heel." She silently advanced around the bend, pulled off a thermal insulated glove to reach inside her goose-down parka, and retrieved the small set of binoculars in an inside pocket. Titan sniffed the air, his nose and ears alerted toward the buildings. His extraordinary sense of smell had picked up something new, something that did not belong.

Thwack. Thwack. The sound of sharp blows echoed across the ice-covered lake beyond the boathouse. Adjusting the focus on the lens, she spied a male figure splitting cordwood behind the three-car garage.

Thwack. Driven by some inner demon, a broad-shouldered man clad only in a white T-shirt and jeans repeatedly raised an axe buried in a log above his head and slammed the end into a stump with a force that shook his lean body. Two pieces of wood catapulted through the air to land in the snow several feet away. The macho demonstration of force triggered memories buried deep. Heart thumping, she fought nausea. Post-traumatic stress, the police shrink called it.

Handsome fiend, she decided, peering through the lens at the stranger's sun-streaked fair hair, well-proportioned six-foot-two frame, and a largish nose under thunderous brows. Still, he had to be unhinged to split wood without a coat in the frigid air given the couple of cords stacked high against the garage wall—enough firewood for two winters.

"This guy looks like trouble, Titan. We don't want trouble." She lowered the binoculars, cursing under her breath. She'd moved to Port Carson to avoid having to deal with "situations."

No way was she approaching this lunatic too close. Not without a weapon. Her left hand slipped into her pocket to clasp the cell phone with 911 on speed dial. Alerted by pheromones in beaded sweat on his mistress's brow under her fur-trimmed hood, Titan's muscles bunched as he prepared to launch at the intruder on her command. Catrina needed to figure out who this guy was before the retired police dog tore a chunk out of his tight butt.

Quickly she dialed her contact for the property, Jenna Jordan's personal assistant.

A decidedly grumpy voice answered the summons. "Who the hell is it?"

"Stacey, it's Catrina Turner up in Muskoka. There's someone in the cottage. Did Jenna give anyone the key and alarm code?"

"Do you realize it is…oh my god, six a.m. here in California?" came the angry retort.

Catrina was well aware of the three-hour time difference. She swallowed impatience. "You hired me for security. I'm checking up because there isn't anyone scheduled to be in residence. The alarm didn't activate, but if it's an intruder, I'm going to call the police."

"NO! Don't call the cops." Catrina heard noises indicating movement—a series of thuds and muffled curses as Stacey scrambled out of bed. "I, um, meant to send an email. It slipped my mind, what with the *Golden Globe Awards* next weekend, the party invitations…Jenna's a nominee. Don't tell her I forgot. She'll have my ass. Not that she cares about anything at the moment except fitting into her designer gown."

"So who's the guest?"

"Chett de Groot."

"Who?"

"The screenwriter. Don't piss him off, or I'll be fired for sure. Jenna loaned him the cottage with the expectation that he'll write a lead part for her into his next project. If she doesn't win a Golden Globe, Chett's her backup plan. Roles for women in their late thirties are in short supply, and her talent agent is trying to convince Jenna, a sex siren, to accept a role as a *mother*. Can you believe it?"

Without waiting for Catrina's response, the words continued to tumble out. "Her fans won't frigging believe it either. She'll be finished. So listen to me closely. Give Chett de Groot *whatever he wants*. Jenna's career depends on it! *Capisce*?"

"Yes, ma'am. Wait—" The call disconnected.

Catrina tucked the phone back into her pocket. "Well, Titan, we've been given our instructions. He's the genuine article. That's it for the excitement today."

Which suited her just fine. Situation averted. After handing in her badge and her Glock, she'd obtained a private investigator license but decided not to apply for a handgun license. She'd built a new life in vacation country specifically to escape criminal violence. On the rare occasion of a break and enter, she called in the Ontario Provincial Police.

If some writer nerd she'd never heard of wanted to hole up alone in a secluded house to write a part for Jenna, she'd see if he needed anything and then leave him to it. No doubt he'd go stir crazy and be booked on a flight back to California within a week.

Her enjoyment of the normally uneventful daily security patrol now spoiled, she trudged the rest of the way down the hill to the six-bedroom "cottage" with four bathrooms, a home theatre, and a formal dining room that sat twelve. The "bunky," a guest house with two additional bedrooms, nestled among the trees a hundred feet farther along the shore.

She plodded stiff-legged toward the man, snowshoes sinking softly into fluffy powder. Thirty feet away she halted. Sensing her apprehension, Titan moved into a protective stance at her left and barked a sharp warning. At the sound, the man she presumed to be Chett de Groot spun on one cowboy boot, axe at the ready in his right hand.

"This is private property," he shouted, red-faced. "Don't come any closer."

Titan scented fear and barked a warning. Adrenaline coursed through Catrina's veins. She inhaled crisp bracing air and fought the urge to backtrack to her nice, safe vehicle. The stranger was cranky and cold, she told herself sternly, not a deranged axe murderer. For the dog's sake, she needed to radiate calm.

"I'm the security hired to protect this place," she shouted back in her best authoritative cop voice. She extracted a business card from a pocket and waved it at him. "Can I have your name?"

"Chett de Groot."

Satisfied, she advanced a few steps to get a closer look at his unshaven, flushed mug and wild eyes. "Do you need anything? A parka, perhaps?"

"No. I just want to be left alone. No women. No dogs. Especially no *dogs*." He gripped the axe handle with two muscular arms and slammed the sharp edge an inch into the stump.

Impressed, and not in a good way, Catrina hastily dropped the card onto the snow.

"Give me a shout if you change your mind. Stacey asked me to help you out." There, she'd done her duty. With Titan heeling tight to her left, she quickstepped up the long driveway like her life depended on it.

"Wait. There's no water."

Pushing back the fur-trimmed hood, she twisted to confront this new complication. "The place is closed up for the winter. The waterlines were drained in case they froze."

Catrina sighed, knowing that it'd be a heck of a job to get the well pump going to supply water to the house during the coldest month of the winter. She knew for a fact that the plumbing contractor had not installed heat trace on the waterlines because the owner had sworn she'd never in a million years set foot in snow unless it was artificial snow in a soundstage.

Perhaps Chett could get by with bottled water and the outhouse. "How long are you staying?"

"Long enough to write a blockbuster screenplay."

She'd read that a movie screenplay only ran about a hundred pages, most of that dialogue. "A week?"

A reluctant grin slashed the darkness contorting his features. "A month, at least." The smile disappeared. "Maybe longer," he admitted.

"You'll need the water, then," she agreed. "The plumber will be on it this afternoon."

"If it's not too much trouble."

The sociable comment threw her. Chett was a real Dr. Jekyll and Mr. Hyde. She cocked her head, considering. This de Groot was either a close friend of Jenna's or an annoyance she wanted as far as possible from LA and the voracious paparazzi during the awards season. It was useless to speculate. Shrugging her shoulders, she decided she'd err on the side of caution and be nice to him.

She rotated her snowshoes and trudged a few steps nearer. "Calling a plumber is part of the comprehensive service I provide to my clients. Besides security, I arrange for renovations and maintenance, landscaping, vehicle repair, and even catering."

Keeping a wary eye on the dog, Chett advanced to pick her business card out of the snow. "Turner and Pooch Security Services?" The barest hint of a smile twitched the corners of his mouth.

"That's us. I'm Catrina Turner." She waved at the dog. "This is Titan. He's a retired police general service dog and great at tracking tourists who get lost in the woods."

Titan gave a happy bark. Chett took a nervous step back. "Does he bite?"

"When provoked."

"Shit." The sweat from the guy's exertions had cooled in the frigid air, and he'd begun to shiver. "I traveled three thousand miles to a place where I can work without any distractions. You and especially that animal don't need to check on the place while I'm living here."

She shook her head. "Oh yes, I do. It's in my contract. Sorry, you're stuck with me for the duration. Titan and I will stay out of your way."

The hypervigilant part of her psyche was super-relieved that he had a dog phobia. If Jenna ever complained that Catrina didn't pay enough attention to Chett de Groot, she had that explanation in her back pocket.

She swiveled in the clumsy foot apparatus in another attempt to leave, another attempt to salvage the rest of her day. For the sake of Jenna's career, and thus her ability to pay for Catrina's services, she only needed to keep Chett comfortable for the duration of his visit.

"Buy a coat and gloves," she suggested over her shoulder. "There's no clause in my contract that covers nursing you through pneumonia."

As she crested the slope before the curve in the lane, she chanced a quick glance backward, saw him watching her.

"Next time bring a leash," he yelled.

★★★★★

Chett heeded the attractive dark-haired security guard, in her early thirties at a guess, and retreated to the warmth of the wood fire blazing in the great room's enormous fieldstone fireplace. Jenna had given him *carte blanche* with respect to the stocked freezer, wine cellar, and bar. The lack of running water was a minor annoyance. He didn't take water in his whisky anyway.

He filled a glass from a half-empty bottle of twelve-year-old golden elixir, shed worn boots, propped sock feet on the distressed pine coffee table in front of the white leather sofa, and contemplated his grim situation.

He needed a hit.

The most recent action film with his name attached went straight to DVD. More importantly, it had lost money. Millions. A-list directors and producers had wasted no time deleting his name from their contact lists. Their assistants pretended to lose his messages.

Compounding his predicament as a washed-up screenwriter at the ripe age of thirty-six, his ex-wife had filed for overdue spousal support. He raised his glass to the hot blond southern princess who'd mutated into the Wicked Witch when the money ran out. *Good luck with that, honey.*

Jenna believed in him. She'd offered him her retreat up in Canada, convinced the lack of distractions would enable him to focus on writing another hit like *Undercover Slasher*, his bad cop thriller of five years ago.

Besides, he owed her. He and Jenna went back fifteen years when both worked in the Beverly Hills Hotel—him behind the bar, her waiting tables. She'd snagged an agent first, got a few walk-ons, and invited him to industry parties as her date. At one party she introduced Chett to a producer who wanted to get into Jenna's pants so bad he agreed to read Chett's screenplay. Eventually the guy dumped Jenna for another ingenue but did option the screenplay.

Jenna had set up his lucky break. He'd sworn on his parents' graves to write a leading role for her.

Of course, he'd neglected to mention his writer's block.

Purchase *Seduced by the Screenwriter* in print or ebook format from Amazon. The ebook is also available from several other distributors. See all buy options at MadelleMorgan.com.

If you enjoyed *Caught on Camera*, please rate it and post an honest review on Goodreads.com or the site where you purchased it. This will help other readers decide to buy the book. A sentence or two in your own words would be fan-tastic and much appreciated!

Books by Madelle Morgan

Diamond Hunter, Romantic Suspense, 2015

Hollywood in Muskoka **Series:**
Caught on Camera, Book 1, Romantic Comedy, 2016
Seduced by the Screenwriter, Book 2, Contemporary Romance, 2017
Hollywood Hero, Book 3, Contemporary Romance, 2021

Upcoming books:
The Executive's Errand, Book 4—Skylar and Wade's story
The Director's Dilemma, Book 5—Asta and Finn's story
The Producer's Passion, Book 6—Tiffany and Garth's story

Subscribe at MadelleMorgan.com for occasional email announcements of new releases, and download *The Next Big Thing*, a free steamy, fun short story.

About the Author

Madelle, three sisters, and assorted cats and dogs enjoyed wonderful summers at their grandparents' cottage on a lake in the District of Muskoka, Ontario, Canada. Muskoka was named by *National Geographic Traveler* magazine as one of their top 20 Best of the World Must-see Places.

Muskoka's rocky shorelines are dotted with palatial properties owned by wealthy families and Hollywood celebrities. At sixteen, being neither rich nor famous, Madelle worked briefly as a chambermaid at the now-closed Delawana Inn, followed by three summers as a general store cashier at Picnic Island Resort in Honey Harbour, on Georgian Bay.

The *Hollywood in Muskoka* series updates the upstairs/downstairs trope: successful people in the film industry on vacation fall for local service providers. The name of the fictional village of Port Carson is a tip of the hat to Carson, the Downton Abbey butler. View Muskoka images that inspired the stories on Pinterest.com/madellem.

Madelle lives in Ottawa, Canada's capital, with her husband and their labradoodle Raven. She dreams of owning a waterfront cottage. Or at least a pool.

Follow Madelle

Amazon.com
Goodreads.com
Pinterest.com/madellem
Twitter.com/madellemorgan
Facebook.com/MadelleMorganAuthor

Made in the USA
Monee, IL
22 June 2026

55535792R00133